Countdown
To Terror

By

Trevor Burton

Acknowledgements

Many thanks to those friends and family who read an unfinished and unedited manuscript, all of whom offered only positive comments and support even though body language and tone conveyed that improvements could be made.

My wife Sue listened tirelessly to my requests for feedback on plot lines and locations, not to mention necessary comments on precisely what females don't wear?

Steve Moyes who produced an excellent cover design at a most favourable rate.

To Detective Constable Sean Stimson and Detective Sergeant Helene Miller Of the MET who after being pressganged into reading the book did not advise of any total howlers in procedural matters.

Finally Professional editor Rebecca Keys who I know even worked at home on the final editing process

Prologue

The pain was intense. It was if two giant clamps were squeezing his stomach from either side. He couldn't sit still or lie down; nor could he stand up. Several faces materialised, peering down at him. 'You'll be fine in a minute. This will help,' one said, as a syringe entered his arm.

The Gent was disorientated. He wasn't in *that place*; there were no guards. It wasn't a bullet this time. It was night-time, so why wouldn't they let him sleep. The pain wasn't so bad now: morphine works, but it messes with your head. Here was another one, in a different colour uniform, 'Just checking your blood pressure, sir'.

'Want to sleep,' he murmured. 'Why won't they let me sleep?'

Six hours later he woke up in a sweat. It had been a nightmare – a flashback. When he'd been rescued from *that place,* they'd said there would be flashbacks. *Post-traumatic stress*, they'd called it; he preferred *friggin' nightmare*. And for some years into the future he would have occasional bouts of serious abdominal pain as small bits of shrapnel decided to move around. Looking about he remembered now! It was May 2012. Last night's nightmare was not about *that place* at all; he was now in his own bed in the converted barn on a South Cheshire farm. Sheila, his new architect girlfriend, was gently nudging him. Last night had merely been a recollection of five days when he had collapsed with a serious bout of abdominal pain and had to be carted off to A&E at South Cheshire Hospital, where, because he had arrived in a car to get there faster, he'd not been considered urgent. He'd been unable to stand, sit or lie down, and had writhed about on the floor of A&E, entertainment for the would-be patients, until eventually they had decided there was space in the resuscitation ward to check him out. A doctor had arrived, accompanied by several different aides in various uniforms. The doctor's cheerful greeting was, 'We're not looking too well, are we, sir?' Five hours later, at midnight, chest shaved, and morphine drip attached and a myriad of questions and tests completed he was moved to a room for the night. Another uniform came in, asking the same questions for another hour. Then at last they'd gone and he could sleep, save for regular hourly visits to check his blood pressure.

Fortunately, the metal eventually moved south and he recovered enough to be let out by lunchtime the next day.

Chapter 1

It is said that the triangle bordered by, Macclesfield, Altrincham and Bramhall in the English county of Cheshire boasts more millionaires per square mile than any other area of the country. The triangle was Samir's territory.

Samir's father was a rich Pakistani, and although short and rotund, he'd possessed enough charm – not to mention cash – to facilitate the pursuit and seduction of a pale-skinned second-generation Pakistani girl of outstanding beauty from Birmingham. Their son Samir was a slim, pale-skinned young man, of average height, but possessing above average looks. With an IQ above 115, he appeared aloof, but actually he just did not care.

Samir had originally been articled to Anders-Lybert Accountants with the intention of being a fast-track high-flyer, but his lack of drive and ambition had made him an unlikely candidate for promotion, and only the connection to his father kept him on the books. With only a nominal salary, he relied on his father's money to sustain him, but for how long?

Halfheartedly still undertaking accountancy studies at Manchester Metropolitan University, Samir was an occasional mosque attendee, which his father silently accepted rather than suffer his non-attendance. Two other fellow young acolytes were also attending MMU, and together they were ideal candidates for grooming by radical Muslims, determined to incite *Jihad*.

It was Friday 30th March, 2012, and Samir was at the mosque in Cheetham Hill, Manchester. Although the family lived in Wilmslow, an affluent town on the south side of Manchester, his father still kept up the habit of attending from the early days when he had first arrived from Pakistan. Samir was observing prayers on this particular Friday – in fact, the very word for Friday in Arabic comes from the name for the special prayer that is done only on that day. He had not been for some time and was getting some flak from his family, which he would normally have just shrugged off, but a special invitee was preaching today: Ibrahim Abelgadar, an immigrant firebrand cleric, originally from Baghdad, Iraq. Also in attendance were Abdullah, and Ali, two of Samir's friends from MMU.

The speaker ranted and raved for forty-five minutes, quoting chapter and verse from the Koran, while Samir went glassy-eyed trying to stay awake.

Chatting together afterwards in an ante room, Ali whispered, 'What about the plan then? Are we going to do something or not?'

Samir remained silent as Abdullah responded, 'Come on, guys, let's be real. Who do we think we are? How do we actually go about something like that? And don't say it's all on the internet.'

Ali continued, 'Well, we find someone who knows how. What about that Hussein bloke, right? He knows, right? Hasn't he been trained and everything, even been on the *Hajj* (pilgrimage) to Mecca?'

Abdullah challenged again, 'My uncle says to steer well clear of him. He's big trouble, and anyway, what do you think, Samir?'

'Well, I agree it's all right talking about it between ourselves, but we don't really know how to go about it, do we?'

There was silence for a while as the problem was mulled over.

'I don't suppose it would do any harm to talk to him,' volunteered Abdullah.

Samir was non-committal, but Ali was all

for it. The seed was sown, and only the time and place remained to be fixed.

The trio caught up with Hussein as he was walking down Cheetham Hill Road towards the centre of Manchester, where most of the buildings were over a hundred years old. The one exception was the old Northern Hospital, which had closed in 1944 and had been pulled down for redevelopment. They passed Asian businesses, an immigration advice centre, and Asian shops with open stalls in front, selling all kinds of produce spilling over onto the pavement.

Samir was nervous. He had been in the company of Hussein only once before. Hussein was in his early thirties, a big, tough-looking man with short hair and a black beard, but it was the eyes – black and soulless, with absolutely no expression – that were most frightening.

The myth about him was only partly true. He *was* hard – very hard. Born in a poor village in Afghanistan, he had been sodomised from an early age by a village elder, which wasn't uncommon in that part of the world, and was still tacitly accepted. He still bore the scars on his back where he had been beaten into submission. Escape came when the Taliban routed the village looking for informers. The training camp had given him everything he needed to survive: food, a cause, martial arts training, and of course indoctrination in the guise of education. He was later assigned to protect senior clerics, and eventually came to the UK with Ibrahim Abelgadar.

The trio chatted as they walked, trying to include Hussein in the small-talk as they continued all the way to Manchester, but he evaded all questions and contributed almost nothing to the conversation.

As they approached a junction, the gang appeared from around a corner – football fans, given the number of scarves worn. They hailed from the New Islington area of Ancoats, and the leader Fwankie (Franklin) whispered to the gang.

'We'll have these Pakis, eh, boys?'

The trio of friends immediately stepped off the kerb ready to cross over or even take flight, but Hussein's pace never missed a beat: he just marched on straight towards them. There was a slight pause as the two bravest came forward in obvious fighting mode, with shoulders twitching and boots at the ready. Hussein marched on, and then suddenly lunged forward and struck with the speed of a cobra: one arm shot out into the face of the thug on his right, the heel of his right hand whacking the nose. There was a sickly cracking noise, and the thug collapsed into the arms of the one behind. Without hesitation, two fingers of Hussein's left hand poked sharply into the eyes of the thug now straight in front, and he too fell, temporarily blinded and in excruciating pain. The gang parted like the Red Sea, and Hussein marched on with the trio now glued to his heels.

Ali was the first to speak 'WOW! That was fantastic! Where did you learn how to fight like that? Training camp?'

The others were also eager to learn more, but Hussein stayed silent as they continued into town with the tower of Strangeways prison visible over the rooftops on the right. As they drew near the Manchester Evening News arena, he stopped and turned.

'We need to meet again, maybe tomorrow, to discuss your plans.'

'How do you know?' they exclaimed in unison.

'You are children,' he replied scornfully. 'Do you really think our meeting today was a coincidence? The imam has known of your intentions all along and was waiting for the visit of the preacher to confirm the final decision that it should go ahead. Ali, give me your mobile number and I will call you tomorrow to meet.'

With that he was off, leaving the trio elated if a little unsure as to how the meeting would turn out. They set off in silence to walk the rest of the way to MMU.

Talking over coffee in a corner of the MMU refectory, the mood was subdued. None of the trio wanted to raise the subject of the plan, and all appeared afraid of Hussein. What had started out as lighthearted and semantic discussion about globalisation and the world being taken over by multinational corporations had somehow morphed into Britain accepting Sharia law and the onward march of Islam into a modern-day Caliphate embracing the Middle East and Europe. Any murkier details as to how this could be achieved had been lost in youthful euphoria. The emergence of Hussein had suddenly and irrevocably moved the goalposts. If they were to meet with Hussein, they would have to show that they were serious, and after recent events they were in no doubt about where this was leading. Each wanted to convince the others that they were heroes, not villains! They parted and went their separate ways, with Ali promising to relay news from Hussein the next day.

Samir had a date with Jenny that evening. He had promised to take her to Bannerman's, the select club in Alderley Edge where he had first picked her up. It had been one of his easier conquests, as it soon became obvious that her confidence needed a boost following the break-up of a long-term relationship, and he was after all a skillful charmer with an apparently wealthy lifestyle. Even though she was a year or two older, it suited Samir as she ticked all the boxes and was relatively undemanding.

Ali and Abdullah met again that evening back at MMU. Samir had originally been enticed to the cause because of his wealth and contacts. He was an easy target for drinks and small loans, and never seemed to mind, knowing full well they had no money. The reason why he was so obliging did not appear to be an issue.

'What do you think this plan is all about, then?' Abdullah said.

'Well, it has to be something big and serious,' Ali countered, 'but precisely what, I don't know.'

'What is the target, then?' Abdullah continued. 'I don't think that's for us to decide, so we'll have to wait for the meeting with Hussein.' They finished their drinks and left for home, Ali promising to relay immediately any news.

The next day he had been on tenterhooks waiting for the call from Hussein. His BlackBerry had played out a rap tune at five thirty-one. It was Abdullah.

'Have you heard anything yet?' he'd enquired.

'No. I would have thought he would have called by now. I've not heard from Samir either, although I think he was out with that new bird of his last night. He doesn't talk much about her, but it was probably somewhere posh as usual. Anyway, it's Saturday and he's a Manchester City fan.'

'You need to leave him alone a bit,' Abdullah advised. 'He does alright by us most of the time. It's just that his head's in the clouds.'

'Yeah, I'm sure you're right. I'll let you know when Hussein calls.'

The call never came on Saturday, Sunday or Monday, by which time the trio had repeatedly called and texted each other. They met up at MMU on the Tuesday.

Abdullah was the first to broach the subject. 'Do you think we should try to contact Hussein?' he asked.

'Problem is we don't really know much

about him or where he is staying. We don't even have a phone number,' replied Ali.

'Perhaps we should wait until Friday and see if he shows up at the mosque,' suggested Samir, even though he didn't relish attending prayers two weeks in a row.

There was instant accord, as though all three were now assessing the inevitable spiral of events that were about to unfold.

Chapter 2

The Gent waiting on platform one at Crewe station on an unusually warm Tuesday, 10th April 2012, would have looked out of place to an interested observer. Most travellers waiting for the West Coast line, Virgin Rail intercity pendolino to London Euston, were professional business-class in slightly crumpled suits, many toting the current fashionable black briefcase-cum-overnight bag slung over the shoulder by a strap. Others were student types in jeans, sporting a rucksack from Sports Direct, alongside a smattering of ethnic minorities, some in traditional garb. Among the fewer passengers waiting at the first-class end of platform one there was the world-weary senior business type and lower-level politicians. With a traditional overnight case and pondering the *Times*, the Gent had the air of a celebrity, dressed in a Ted Baker mid-blue two-piece suit, except for an air of absent-minded detachment.

Ho hum, the train was fifteen minutes late. Finding his seat, he made himself comfortable and settled in to complete the *Times* crossword. After a pleasant and uneventful journey, he took the Northern line to King's Cross and changed to the Piccadilly line to Russell Square, where he walked the short distance to the Imperial Hotel, Bloomsbury, in the heart of Central London.

To the right of the hotel on Southampton row was the old Pitman Training Centre (from Sir Isaac Pitman, the famous inventor of shorthand). Reception was through an archway, where the first view was of a central fountain behind which was a casino. On the right, two groups of statues lined the entrance to the underground car park. There were six life-sized, scantily-clad allegorical women, two of whom were clutching books helpfully entitled *Literature* and *Chemistry*. Another one was clutching a mask indicating *Theatre,* but the other three weren't telling. Reception was on the left.

The assistant manager, remembering him from previous visits, asked, 'How are things in Cheshire, sir? And what are we up to this time?'

'Oh, this and that, but firstly I'm booked in on the Ancient Egypt tour at two thirty in the British Museum,' remarked the Gent.

'Your room is number twenty-four, sir, but it is just being finished off. Can I get you a coffee in the lounge for a few minutes?'

After finishing his coffee, he took the lift to the second floor. After settling in the room, he spent a few moments appreciating the view over Russell Square. Later, pondering his surroundings as one does when closeted in a hotel bathroom, and tiring of counting the number of tiles in the middle of the wall above the basin, his gaze caught something placed awkwardly on the top of the soap dispenser. The object was a credit card, obviously mislaid by the last occupant. He would return it to reception.

After drying his hands, he picked up the card and turned it over to find the words *HELP*, with *museum* written in toothpaste on the black metallic strip on the back of the card. The name on the card was Ms. Carol Lomas. How bizarre; his mind caricatured an effeminate character in the latest TV soap. An hour later he was still pondering the credit card as his curiosity began to build. The card must have been there when he checked in mid-morning, but he hadn't noticed. Why *museum*? He was due there at two thirty on a guided tour, but how would the cardholder know that, and why on earth should she seek him out for help? Was she in danger? Should he call the police? The word *museum* was obviously written on the credit card for a reason!

The Gent's analytical mind was at once

aroused, and what was to have been a short trip to London to visit the British Museum was to turn into a tangled web of intrigue.

The Gent was not short of a bob or two, but after a costly divorce his confidence and ego were still not sufficiently repaired to venture back into the love stakes. Friends and relatives were always trying to fix him up with ideal dates, but when their faces morphed into that of his ex, that was the end of that. Attempts at internet dating usually resulted in one-sided contests with swamp monsters from the inner cities of Manchester and Stoke-on-Trent. For his next venture, he was going to try out the Cheshire Dining Club.

Meanwhile, he consoled himself and kept his considerable intellect alive with occasional short holidays such as this intended visit to the British Museum.

A Cambridge graduate in English with experience in human resources for a multinational company, he was reasonably well travelled and could fit into most social situations. He wasn't the most accomplished athlete, but his golf swing was above average.

He lived in a converted barn and kept chickens and two pigs in half an acre of land, and was fortunate in that the farmer's wife and teenage daughter were happy to look after them all when he was away. He drove an old Saab 900I – one of the last to be manufactured, reflecting Saab's original aeroplane design principles. Maintenance was fastidious and it was kept in concourse condition.

Chapter 3

Sporting a little black dress with bare legs ending in fashionable red high-heeled shoes, Jenny Lomas was standing in the queue at reception in the Imperial Hotel, almost glued to Samir, who was not letting her out of his sight for the merest instant, when she heard a voice she knew but could not immediately place.

The urbane gent only feet away was chatting to the assistant manager and confirming that he had travelled down to London from Crewe, in Cheshire. She was now terrified and paranoid about what Samir might be involved in. He seemed to be spending more and more time with his mates from the college, most of who appeared to be Muslim and certainly did not look like accountancy students. Could she just up and run, go to the police, or confide in her mother? A myriad of thoughts passed through her brain in a matter of seconds as she stood trembling and listening to the gent chatting calmly away to the assistant manager.

Ah, golf, she thought. After breaking up with her prospective Conservative candidate boyfriend, who'd gone off with a political researcher three months earlier, she had been down in the dumps and had fallen for the obvious but insincere charms of Samir – well, obvious in her mother's eyes, anyway. As a way of sparking Jenny back into her old self, her mother had paid for golf lessons at the Forest View Golf Club, where she was a member. Forest View was very friendly, definitely not a stuffy, toffee-nosed, invitation-only kind of place. The golf pro Billy Wills was amusing with an easygoing style, and Jenny made good progress in the beginners group, where surprisingly there were quite a few younger girls learning, ranging from secretaries to an airline pilot.

Carol Jennifer Lomas, known as Jenny to her friends, had chosen Jenny as her preferred mode of address ever since being teased at school that Carol was also a boy's name.

It came to her in a flash. She had turned up at the tee for a round with Billy to sort out her chipping, and Billy had suggested a *lob wedge* – whatever that was – but the reception clerk at the club had come running out to advise that Billy Wills' car had broken down. The gent standing three feet away at the Imperial Hotel reception desk was the Good Samaritan who had been waiting for the next tee time and offered to guide her round if Jenny did not mind. Mind?, It turned out to be excellent: he was a true gentleman and she now knew what a lob wedge was for, even if she could not make it do what it was designed to do.

'Samir, I have left my mobile in the room!' Jenny cried as she sprinted away through the lobby to the lift. The journey in the lift was torture and seemed endless. Could Samir check out and get back to their recently vacated room twenty-four before her? Finding her Good Samaritan again was one thing, but what next? It was only a few weeks ago, so surely he would remember her, but how to make contact without Samir noticing? She had overheard he was to visit the British Museum on a guided tour about Ancient Egypt at two thirty in room sixty-four – the very same venue for Samir's reconnoitre and Islamic study that afternoon. Jenny returned to reception and was mightily relieved to see Samir still settling the bill. The gent was nowhere to be seen.

'I found it next to the TV remote,' she stammered, and Samir grunted something in exasperation. She had got away with it!

Standing in the queue waiting to check out, Samir recalled the events of the past few weeks. He was sweating. Could he keep this up? He was sure Jenny suspected he was up to something: the story he had fed her about further research into Islamic history had not sounded at all convincing, even when he explained that he needed to visit the British

Museum before April 15th, which was when the exhibition *Hajj: Journey to the Heart of Islam* was due to end.

Following the incident with Hussein, the trio had agreed to do nothing until the following Friday prayers when they might bump into Hussein again naturally. They were not to be disappointed: he was waiting for them at the end of prayers and ordered them into a back room. The imam was also there, and lost no time.

'You have been chosen by Ibrahim Abelgadar for a special mission. He is aware of your progress over the last few months, and is impressed.' The trio positively shone with pride at this praise. 'We have further preparations to make, and your leader will be Hussein. You will obey him at all times. Are you ready for this mission?'

Ali and Abdullah, still the most fervent, answered immediately, 'Yes, we are ready, imam!'

Samir, trembling inside and wondering how it had got this far, stammered a moment later, 'Yes, I am ready, imam, but what is the mission?'

'All will be told to you at the right time, but first you, Samir, have two tasks to perform. The first is to visit the British

Museum in London and check out how such a revered institution is kept secure, and the second: in order to finalise your Islamic studies, you must report on *Hajj: Journey to the Heart of Islam*, a special exhibition currently on show there.'

Hussein now addressed the trio: 'From now on, be careful – especially you, Samir, on your mission. We know there are informers who could be watching us and also government agents. I will meet with you again next week after prayers.'

Evidently dismissed, the three left to return to MMU in central Manchester. The atmosphere between them was electric, with all vying to voice the first questions.

It was Abdullah on this occasion, all fired up after the imam's praise. 'Why London though? Why the British Museum? What is the plan? Is it a bomb? Are we going to die?' The words tumbled out furiously.

'Chill mate, chill mate,' his fellow conspirators responded together.

Ali got his oar in first, 'let's just think about it for a while... I wonder if it's something to do with this special exhibition. Could be some VIP is attending and we'd have to kidnap him and hold him to ransom?'

Samir at last was able to contribute, 'The problem there would be that it would end up being a siege.'

Ali, never the sharpest knife in the drawer, was ecstatic, 'Hey! We'd be on the TV with a negotiator and all that!'

Abdullah was more circumspect. 'And we'd end up getting shot by M19.'

The mood quickly descended and they became silent for a while.

'Why me, and what's so special about this exhibition?' Samir wondered.

Abdullah responded with: 'It's obvious, isn't it? You've got dosh, and if you took Jenny along you'd just look like any other tourists. You could even chew gum and pretend to be American.'

'Ha, ha, very funny,' Samir grunted. 'But I suppose there is some logic to that. With Ali's build and that beard he wouldn't get through the front gate.'

At this point they appeared to have convinced each other of the noble aspirations of the venture, and that Samir's tasks were a bit of a holiday – a walk in the park, even.

However, by the time he got home to his apartment on the Alderley Edge side of

Wilmslow, a short distance from his parents' house, Samir was really stressed. He downed a beer and waited for Jenny – good shag would soon sort him out. When she arrived, it was obvious that he was in a bit of a state. She was hardly through the door before he started to drag her clothes off.

'OK!' she cried. 'Give me time to get my breath!' Samir had an animal look and started to raise his hand. 'Look, I warned you before: you hit me again and I'm off for good.' He calmed down immediately but was naked before they even reached the bedroom.

The sex was ardent, physical and furious, and she orgasmed several times.

'Fuckin' 'ell, Samir, what have you been on today?' she asked afterwards, staring down at him as he now languished like a beached dolphin. Whatever had troubled him had disappeared, for the moment at least.

The following day, Samir was at his parents' house for dinner. The house was large: six-bedroomed and with a sweeping gravel drive where the obligatory his-and-hers Mercedes stood shining in the pale sunlight. The wealth came from their fabrics business,

Mansoor Khan Import & Export, based in Strangeways, Manchester, with one of its main customers a well-known high-street retail chain.

Samir's mother Aisha was wearing a chef's blue-striped apron over a western-style flowery summer dress and Scholl sandals as she prepared food in the kitchen, affording Samir the opportunity of talking to his father Mansoor about his impending visit to London. His father listened with some interest, and they discussed the merits of going on the *Hajj*, Mansoor then stating that he too must get around to it one day, before remarking, 'You could call in on your uncle Sulamain while you are down there.'

'Is he still doing that security job at Harrods?' asked Samir.

'You know very well it is not just any security job. He is head of security, which in a place like Harrods is some job. What you might not know is that he was head-hunted for the position after retiring from the Met.'

'Yeah, I know.' Samir had initially lodged with his uncle while studying business at the University of London, Birkbeck College. He did not wish to reveal that he was in touch with his uncle much more often than his father realised, for reasons other than normal family matters.

The British Museum in Great Russell Street, Bloomsbury, Central London, was one of the best value-for-money sites in all London, as entry was FREE!

The Gent was excited as he strolled in bright sunshine the short distance to the main entrance.

As he wandered through the gates, what was most surprising was the absence of any obvious signs of security, save for a uniformed officer with a slightly befuddled air. There were no turnstiles or bag-check; the way into the courtyard was wide open, and inside were a great many people milling about, including lots of school parties.

The entrance appeared dim after the bright sunshine outside. Immediately on the left were the old south stairs, and on the right the Grenville Room. He passed through into the Great Court, which was bathed in light from a beautiful atrium dating from the millennium year 2000 and dedicated to Queen Elizabeth II. He made his way apprehensively up the left stairs to level one, where right and left stairs meet the Court Restaurant. Proceeding through rooms fifty to fifty-three, he arrived in room sixty-four in good time.

There were a few tourists milling around,

but no one who looked remotely like a guide. He wandered a few yards into room sixty-four, trying to adopt the guise of an academic about his work, but his mind was obviously concentrated elsewhere.

He turned back and spotted a man in his early thirties in typical lecturer's garb gathering a large group around him. The group was a mix of tourists, mainly American, a few Japanese, and the rest predominantly English.

At first glance, the identity of credit-card holder Carol Lomas was impossible to determine.

'Ladies and gentlemen,' the guide proclaimed, holding aloft an old-fashioned walking stick with a pink pompom attached to the top. 'This tour will last approximately thirty to forty minutes, and is an introduction to early Egypt. Rapid advances in the technology and social organisation of Egypt during the fifth millennium BC produced a material culture of increasing sophistication. Further innovations followed in about 3100 BC, when the separate predynastic peoples of upper and Lower Egypt were united under a single ruler.'

The Gent would normally have found the narration of great interest, but on this occasion it became merely a drone.

Carol Jenny Lomas was in turmoil. Her life had become stale, and she was involved with a man she no longer knew, whose behaviour had become increasingly odd. She could not believe the story about Islamic studies at the temporary exhibition in the British Museum, but she was relieved that Samir had not insisted she accompany him to the exhibition, instead allowing her to visit room twenty-seven, featuring early Mexican and Mayan culture.

She and Samir had holidayed in Cancun, Mexico, earlier in the year, at the time of the Equinox, and had been fascinated by the ancient Mayan culture, especially the pyramid at Chichen Itza. They had seen the apparition of a serpent descending the steps, caused by the sun's rays, a phenomenon only occurring at the spring and autumn solstice. In fact, Samir had been greatly amused when Jenny was overcome with vertigo at the top of the pyramid and had to descend backwards down steps on the right side, holding onto a rope for support. He'd taken a snapshot to prove it!

Samir at last paid the bill. They stored their baggage and then headed out of the hotel. Jenny now had a problem, for she knew that the Ancient Egypt tour did not begin until two thirty that afternoon, and she had to be sure she would still be in the museum at that time.

'Samir,' she purred, 'you know I said I would buy you lunch, but first can we can go to Waterstones bookshop on Gower Street? It's not very far. I promised my mother I would buy her Nigella's latest recipe book, as it's her birthday on Sunday.'

'Well, OK then, but I need to spend a couple of hours in the museum before heading to Euston.'

'Oh, you're an angel,' she purred again. Jenny was surprised at how easy it was, probably because he was so preoccupied with his own thoughts.

They arrived at the museum at ten minutes to two and agreed to text in about an hour. *Phew!* She thought. '*That should give me time to pick up enough information about Mayan culture and find the gent as well*.

Jenny spent the next fifteen minutes constantly looking at her watch, anxious not to miss spotting the gent, but then became completely engrossed in the minutiae of ancient Mexico. Glancing down at her watch, it was two forty-five. Panicking, she picked up as many leaflets as she could find and hurried to find room sixty-four.

In room sixty-four, a line of ancient

Egyptian statues looked down impassively as an attractive young woman in a little black dress over fashionable pastel leggings with red high heels approached a man in his mid-thirties. He was dressed in smart but casual style, and was hanging on to the back of a tour group peering into the sarcophagus of Agamemnon III.

As the woman came closer, the gent turned and with a double-take exclaimed, 'Jenny! What on earth are you doing here?' There was a flash of understanding as he produced a credit card from his pocket. 'You're Carol Lomas!' he exclaimed. 'But what was the name on the card?'

'Shush, I just didn't know who else to turn to, and when I saw you this morning in the queue at reception I panicked. I mean, you always seemed so calm and clever. It's Samir... my boyfriend. He's into something and I'm scared that he's out of his depth – the strange phone calls and texts on his BlackBerry, and he's nervous and jittery all the time and won't let me out of his sight. Oh, shit! I think I've said too much.'

'Hey, OK. Slow down and let me think for a moment. This is obviously not the right place to talk, so where will you be later?'

'I've to meet Samir shortly and we have a train to catch from Euston early evening.'

'Ah, OK. Give me your mobile number, then, and I'll call you tomorrow. Perhaps we can meet up and you can tell me all about it.'

Jenny was most relieved that her dilemma had been partially revealed to someone and who better than to her Good Samaritan. 'Oh, thank you, thank you!' she stammered. 'You will call, won't you?'

'Yes, of course I will.'

Jenny waved as she turned and walked away, and the Gent could only watch with a mixture of emotions as Jenny disappeared through a crowd of chattering schoolchildren. He couldn't be sure, but he had that nagging feeling that he was being watched. Or was he just being influenced by Jenny's real or imagined thoughts?

Samir, meanwhile, had also been busy, trying to forget his misgivings about the real purpose of his visit. The exhibition was staged in what had been the reading room of the British Library. The pilgrimage to Mecca, the *Hajj*, is the supreme expression of global Islam, and that year, 2012, two and half million Muslims from all over the world would undertake the journey. Pilgrimage was not unique – what set it apart from other religious traditions, including Judaism and Christianity, was that it was a binding obligation for all able-bodied believers who

31

could afford it.

Pilgrims began by going seven times around the Ka'aba, approaching as close to the black stone within it. The route was along a corridor taken by Abraham's exiled concubine Hagar, who drank water from the Well of Zamzam, which saved her life and that of her son Ismail.

Saudi Arabia cooperated with the British museum in staging the exhibition. As guardians of Mecca and its fellow holy city Medina, the Saudis took their responsibility seriously. The prevailing orthodoxy in Saudi Arabia was Sunni, and this gave rise to Shia pilgrims complaining of discrimination when attempting to perform prayers according to Shia rites. This was understandable given the political dimension with Shia Iran. More Shias visited Shia shrines in Iraq than Mecca.

After an hour or so of absorbing these and a myriad of other facts that he thought would impress the imam back home, Samir felt in need of Zamzam water or some similar refreshment. Texting Jenny, he arranged to meet her at the Court Restaurant on level one. Over coffee they chatted about each other's projects. Samir appeared much more relaxed, and rest of the afternoon passed without incident before they set off for Euston and the journey home.

The Gent persevered with the rest of the Ancient Egypt tour, but later, back in his hotel room, he remembered little. His mind was pondering the doubts and fears Jenny had expressed about Samir. Was she being over-imaginative, or was there something more to it? Frustrated, he checked out of the Imperial Hotel and caught the last train back to Crewe.

He spent a restless night, and awoke the next day none the wiser. He decided to leave it nearer to lunchtime before making the call to Jenny

Chapter 4

The Gent paced around his conservatory eating extra-strong peppermints as he pondered what could be behind Jenny's outburst yesterday. He stared intently into the garden, not even noticing the antics of squirrels as they scurried about finding nuts, something he normally would have found amusing. Still emotionally bruised from his divorce, he was arrogant but not conceited, and realized that he was quite excited at the prospect of spending time with Jenny – and not just for the opportunity of helping her with her dilemma.

At quarter past twelve, he picked up the phone. The salutations were a little awkward at first.

'I wasn't sure you would call,' she said.

'No problem,' he replied. 'Have you come up with any more ideas as to what could be going on? I mean, it did seem rather strange and farfetched as you described it yesterday, if you don't mind me saying so.'

There was a pause before Jenny responded, 'I know you think I'm imagining things, and he does seem much more relaxed now that we've come back, but I still think there is something going on. I haven't imagined it all – the text messages and strange calls and everything.'

'Right, OK, then, what about if we meet face to face and see if we can make more sense of it between us? Can you get up to the golf club later, say five thirty?'

'Oh yes, sure, that would be great. I'll see you there then.' With that Jenny was gone, leaving the Gent still pacing and pondering.

He arrived at Forest View Golf Club at twenty-five past five to find Jenny sitting at a table by the window, wearing a smart cream Arran sweater with blue jeans and black casual shoes, nursing a gin and tonic. Raising a hand in greeting, he went up to the bar and ordered the same. There was no hint of understanding as the barman respectfully performed his task but a knowing smile touched his lips as the Gent sat down and poured his tonic into Bombay Sapphire gin over ice and lime.

The place was otherwise empty so to an observant barman the smiles from the only occupied table could have been those of lovers rather than co-conspirators. They sipped their gins and it was Jenny who broke the silence first.

'Thank you for coming and treating me as normal. I know it must seem silly.'

'Not at all, I'm delighted that you chose to confide in me,' the Gent responded. 'You've told me about strange calls and text messages, but not what you think they are all about. Do you have any inkling about what it is that may be getting Samir so uptight?'

Jenny looked thoughtful for a moment and then went into full flight.

'Well, he is a bit of a playboy – knows all the right clubs and that, and could have any girl he fancied, really – but I don't think he's bad in any great sense, perhaps just easily led. Over the last few weeks he seems to meet with his Muslim friends more and more, and when I ask him what they talk about he just clams up. But I've seen some of the texts, and they say things like, "Where is it going to be? And what exactly are we going to do?" At first they just seemed to be trying to save the world, but then they are younger than him – about twenty – and he's now twenty-four. Only four years younger than me, so you'd think he would have grown out of all that idealism by now. He did say that a few weeks ago a new visiting imam had been preaching at the mosque, and since then he has become more moody and withdrawn.'

As Jenny paused for breath, the Gent took

the opportunity to speak. 'It definitely seems to me that there's been an escalation in events, what with the visit to London. Why did Samir have to go not the others?'

Jenny came straight back with, 'That's interesting. I caught something about that when he was off-guard after... well, we'd had a drink or two... and it seems that the other two wouldn't look right and of course they don't have Samir's money, or dare I say it, me, to take along.'

'Yes, that does kind of fit together when you consider it all, and from what you've told me he certainly doesn't look like a terrorist. What I can't understand, though, is why this preacher or whoever would send a group from Manchester to London. And why target the British Museum, which displays Islam in a good light, I think? Can I chew this over for a while and perhaps have an off-the-record chat with an old friend of mine, an inspector in the Greater Manchester Police.'

A bit rattled, Jenny added, 'You will be careful, though?'

'Yes, of course I will – no names mentioned all hypothetical. And I've just had an idea: would it be useful if I could meet Samir when I just happen to bump into you both at Bannerman's or somewhere?'

'Yes, OK, that sounds good. I'll let you know when we will be there next.'

With that the conversation passed into golf-speak as they finished their drinks.

The next day, the Gent was back at Forest View Golf Club perusing the competitions board. He did not play competitions regularly, which was unfortunate as he had a mid-range handicap and would inevitably improve with a little more practice. He found the name he was looking for: Bill Lambert, the self-same inspector in the GMP. The competition on the following Wednesday 18th April, a week later, was an eighteen-hole Stableford competition, with groups of three players. The names were entered in pencil, and he rubbed two names out and inserted them in a blank line above, hoping no one would notice. Stupid! This was a golf club, and there would be uproar, but he would just have to ride it out if discovered.

On the 18th, the inspector arrived in good time, and the pleasantries continued for a few minutes. The inspector asked him about his divorce and his success in the romance game – answer: sweet FA, which he freely admitted was more to do with himself as his potential lovers. He enquired after the inspector's family and how the eldest son Denis was doing on his first tour in Iraq. The reply was chastening in that having survived a car bomb whilst on patrol two months before, Denis was still in hospital.

There was a period of silence whilst putting the first hole and driving off the second, except of course for the obligatory 'good shot', and 'robbed' etc. The real business began on the long fairway to the fourth hole.

The Gent began hesitantly, 'Bill, if I were to ask you a hypothetical question, off the record, would you be able to give me a hypothetical answer? For example, if there were an Islamic terrorist cell operating in Manchester, why would they be sent down to London, and why do you think the target would be a great institution of the arts given that this is Olympic year?'

The inspector paused for thought in order to craft his reply. 'I can see that although it is fifteen years since we were at Sandhurst together, studying military strategy, you've lost none of your guile in boxing with the enemy whilst allowing a little wiggle room for negotiation... Well! As it's off the record and even if it is two questions, here goes: firstly, as you would expect in Olympic year, there is a great deal of security in place with half our armed forces in or around London and warships sailing up the Thames. This is just the headline-grabbing overt stuff, never mind the covert stuff going on behind the scenes. The straight answer to the first question is that all known potential types are being monitored very closely, and hopefully wouldn't even get close to a target with a sparkler right now. This would explain why a group from up North would stand a much better chance of remaining undetected. In answer to the second question, they would be looking for some kind of high-profile target to maximise media exposure, but security at the Olympics should be tighter than a drum.'

The Gent waited patiently whilst the inspector took a drop from a water hazard on the sixth, deciding not to comment when he used his extra two-inch length custom-made driver (he was six feet four inches tall) to measure the two club lengths allowed, away from the hazard to make the drop. 'Thanks for that, Bill. It all seems quite logical when you put it that way. Let's just hope hypothesis never moves to action.'

'I'm sure I don't need to need to remind you of my hotline number just in case.'

In the nineteenth hole, three and a half hours later over a pint of Speckled Hen, the mood was jolly with the usual banter with other golfers who all claimed they were playing great until the eighteenth hole. The inspector was in especially good spirits, as he had beaten the Gent by five clear points, something he had never come close to achieving before.

Three days later, on Saturday 21st, the Gent was pacing his conservatory, and pondering again how to smooth his way into the in-crowd at Bannerman's without appearing out of place. He needed a companion. Amelia, his ex-wife's younger sister, looked no older than Jenny, and although their relationship was purely platonic she had been his partner before in situations where an escort was a distinct advantage. A startling redhead, she was a lesbian with a live-in partner, but the opposite of obvious, and would be the ideal choice for the mission in hand. Still getting to grips with his new BlackBerry, he was pleased when his call proved successful at the first attempt, and was amused by her good-humored greeting.

He was just about to speak when he realised it was actually a recorded message. Amelia should consider voice-overs; she was a natural.

She called back later that day and was not surprised that it was another covert mission. He explained that the aim was to suss out

Jenny's boyfriend Samir, and she agreed immediately, confirming that she was free both Friday and Saturday of the following weekend. Once he knew which day, he would call round for a drink first and explain the situation in more detail.

Chapter 5

Two young members of the football gang injured by Hussein were now out of the care of the local outpatients department and, whilst still mentally scarred, were starting to venture out and meet their fellow gang members again. They had yet to rejoin any nefarious activities.

What they had only recently discovered, though, was that on the day of the incident two other, clearly more resourceful members of the gang had followed Hussein. They had trailed him from Cheetham Hill Road, over the bridge behind Victoria railway station, down Corporation Street to the big wheel. Opposite the entrance to the Arndale Shopping Centre, the big wheel stood on the site of the area bombed by the Provisional Irish Republican Army (IRA) on 15th June 1996 in an attack that targeted the city's infrastructure and caused widespread damage. Two hundred and twelve people were injured, but there were no fatalities.

Upon entering the Arndale Shopping Centre Hussein became twitchy; this sixth sense had kept him alive on many occasions.

He wandered the malls for a few minutes, stopping at a Costa coffee shop to check things out. He was too good an operator to miss the young scumbags following him and trying not to look obvious. Deliberately pausing to look in a few shop windows, he led them through the lower level of the Arndale, then making a right turn he continued through TK Maxx, up the escalator and out into Market Street. At the top he crossed the Metrolink tram lines to Piccadilly, and then followed the tram lines to the right, and after traversing what was Piccadilly Gardens before it was concreted over, he crossed over the bus station and through the Piccadilly Tower arch, knowing this area was normally devoid of people, thus affording his followers nowhere to hide. They had to linger until Hussein exited the other side, then he darted across the street to the right and then down into George Street, where he quickly disappeared in the small side streets and alleyways of Chinatown.

Pressured by other gang members and parents, and with an eye on compensation, the injured members finally made a complaint at Bootle Street police station. The description of the assailant was duly logged, but no one appeared too hopeful of a result, especially as it was thought the injured thugs probably got what was coming to them.

Samir was bored. He was staring out of the window overlooking the River Mersey, which was swollen with water running down from the major river valleys of the Pennines. It was still was raining hard, as it had been all that week, and it was only Wednesday. He counted the arches of the Stockport viaduct – all twenty-seven of them, at the time of its construction it was the largest viaduct in the world, and it remained one of Western Europe's biggest brick structures. He was on a job with the audit senior of Anders-Lybert Accountants, a small engineering works in Stockport. The job was coming to an end, and now that he came to think about it, maybe the company as well. He had reconciled the bank account the day before, and the overdraft was even worse now than last year. It had risen steadily over the last eighteen months as the recession deepened until it was again over the agreed limits. The bank, one of those bailed out by the taxpayer, would not lend any more cash despite all the overtures from Prime Minister David (call-me-Dave) Cameron and Chancellor of the Exchequer George Osborne to banks in general to assist small business. "We are all in it together," had been Cameron's rousing cry at election time, but some like the family shareholders of CF

Fabrication Engineers were in it deeper than most. Chairman Cyril Fordspike had nothing left to mortgage, and the continuing attacks on pension schemes left no hope there. It was showing in his demeanour and his regular hangovers. Cyril and audit partner Nils Lybert were due to meet with the bank again the following week at their palatial offices in Spinningfields, a new development in the central financial district of downtown Manchester. There was not much hope around Stockport at the moment; many small firms were going bust and the central part of the town looked dilapidated, with more charity shops and to-let signs appearing each week.

The senior had gone out to lunch with the director, leaving Samir to work on his own. They had attended the stock-taking that morning, an exciting project to rival that of snail-racing, left-handed angle brackets, right-handed hanging brackets, widgets and wodgets galore.

Samir yawned again, and forced himself to look down upon the scintillating charms of the company's corporation tax computation. He tried again, for probably the fourth time. He looked up last year's file to no avail: it might as well have been in Chinese. He wished now that he had paid more attention in classes at Manchester Metropolitan University, but the lecturer on taxation was hardly charismatic –

frankly awful, in fact: bald and myopic, with a huge belly overhanging cheap trousers. He prefaced every topic with, "when I was an Inspector at Her Majesty's Revenue and Customs – Inland Revenue, as it was known then – well, I could tell you a thing or two, I'll say!" Samir heard voices, and began to scribble feverishly.

Chapter 6

It was Saturday 28th April and early evening. The Gent backed the green Saab out of the barn and enjoyed the few miles' drive in the pale sunshine to Amelia's cottage. She made drinks: Bombay Sapphire gin and tonic with ice and lime. She looked stunning in an azure-blue trouser suit over a pure white vest-top, and was quick to comment on his sartorial choice of a light beige Ted Baker suit with a maroon shirt worn open without a tie. They would look the part at Bannerman's.

After enquiring about her sister – his ex – and receiving no untoward reply or significant update about her own personal life, she broached the purpose of their venture that evening.

'So you've given me some info about this female golfing friend, but not why we need to go out clubbing and pretending to be an item. You don't normally go out of your way to make your dates jealous; you just generally mess up, period.'

'Thanks for the vote of confidence,' he countered. 'Actually, it's her boyfriend I'm trying to suss out. She thinks he is behaving strangely and could be deep into something he can't get out of.'

'Well, why do you have to get involved anyway?' Amelia shot back. 'Unless of course you do really fancy her, it's about time you found a girlfriend; you can't sulk forever.'

'Yes, yes, I know, you're right, but the purpose tonight is to figure it out if she is letting her mind run away or if he really is up to something dodgy, in which case I would have to have a chat with someone else.'

Amelia responded with a withering look. 'Someone else... you can be obtuse sometimes. It's no wonder Mary divorced you.'

Picking up his jacket, he ended the conversation. 'I just need to delve a little into his personality, that's all. Let's go, shall we?'

The drive over to Alderley Edge was uneventful, and they returned to their normal composure with the odd bout of good-humored banter. The car park was completely full when they arrived, with bouncers waving people away before they could even try to enter. Driving over the bridge into the village proper, they tried the first car park serving a supermarket and row of other retail outlets. That was also full. Eventually they found a place in a long-stay car park further up in the village.

Bannerman's was heaving with the usual sprinkling of footballers and television celebrities. The music for the night was all Bee Gees, dedicated to Robin Gibb who had sadly died a few days earlier from cancer. Jenny was nowhere to be seen, so after purchasing drinks they fought their way through the scrum at the bar to a quieter corner where Amelia had a spotted a friend in a group of half a dozen revellers. The mood was jovial, and he soon became immersed in a conversation with Tim, a junior newsreader with the BBC at their new centre at Media City on Salford Quays, and Charlotte, a budding partner in a Manchester firm of chartered accountants. He kept up with the conversation through topics ranging from the Euro collapse and the sex scandals of Berlusconi, but could only nod sagely when the discussion drifted into which country would lose its triple A-rated Moody credit rating status.

He eventually spotted Jenny in a small group, and whispered to Amelia before guiding her over to make the engineered 'surprise' encounter.

Jenny saw him walking over and on cue offered a warm greeting.

'Hi, I didn't know this was your kind of

place,' she said, turning and introducing the others in the group before finally including Samir.

'It was Amelia's birthday yesterday,' the Gent replied.

He was immediately struck by Samir. He had imagined a stereotype of studious Islamic scholar complete with beard, but here stood a lithe, athletic figure with matinee-idol looks. It was obvious that Jenny and other girls would consider him attractive. Suppressing a twinge of jealousy, he remained silent for a while whilst covertly studying the group, especially Samir, whose conversation was light, easy, and non-confrontational. Things were indeed becoming more interesting.

He bought a round of drinks, making a mental note that Samir was not teetotal and clearly enjoyed Scotch on the rocks. His opportunity came when Samir asked how he knew Jenny.

'Oh, from the golf club where we are both members and occasionally bump into each other in competitions – and of course the nineteenth hole. Jenny's golf is really coming on. And how did you meet?'

'She was in here one night with friends and we just got chatting.'

I bet you did, he thought.

He continued to glean more about Samir's lifestyle and background, and as they discussed more worldly issues, the Gent volunteered snippets of his own, including his consultancy work for companies undertaking construction projects in the Middle East.

Samir confirmed his interest in Islam and his support for Manchester City, especially since their beating United for the League title this season, their first League title win since 1968. City had gone from strength to strength since their move in 2003 to the Etihad stadium. He skillfully evaded giving any meaningful detail about his employment and accountancy studies, and future plans.

The Gent was forming the distinct opinion that there was a great deal more to Samir than met the eye. A terrorist plotter though? He thought not, but what then?

The club became louder and packed as more revellers poured in after normal pub closing time looking for a glimpse of celebrities. Meaningful conversation was impossible, lost and forgotten in an alcoholic fugue.

The Gent drove (he probably shouldn't have) Amelia home, negotiating the quiet country lanes with precision. He slept in her spare room, leaving any comment till the morning. He woke remarkably fresh, unlike Amelia, who was a tad grumpy and still in robe and slippers but enthusiastically frying eggs and bacon nonetheless. They soon set about debating the events of the night before.

Amelia began, 'That Samir bloke is a bit of a smoothie. I can see why Jenny likes him. Are you sure your judgment isn't clouded because you're jealous? What are you going to do about it, then? And by the way, what's wrong with Samir? He seemed OK to me. I can't see what Jenny would have to worry about, and it's about time you moved on. It's not as if there are kids to consider. You do know that Mary is going out with an airline pilot now? They are currently on holiday in Barbados.'

The Gent was relieved that Amelia had not pushed him on Samir's strange behaviour and what motives could be behind it, this being the main reason for their visit to the club the previous evening.

'I think jealous may a bit over the top, and no, I knew nothing about an airline pilot. At least if he is a millionaire she might stop trying to get more money from me.'

They finished breakfast and discussed other more mundane topics before he was able to depart to muse on his findings, and after thanking Amelia wholeheartedly he drove away deep in thought.

Arriving home, he parked the Saab, and changed into blue overalls and Hunter Wellington boots, and went to feed the pigs and hens, only to find they had already been catered for courtesy of Lily the farmer's daughter. The hens were simple, and didn't ask for much. His favourite, Doris, jumped up, and he caught her for a few seconds almost like you would a cat. The hens never failed to amuse him. How could you get annoyed with a hen, especially when they gave you free eggs and so much tastier than the ones from Tesco? He checked the state-of-the-art stainless steel gravity water feeder. This was apparently meant be a simple device consisting of a container similar to a milk churn in an open circular bowl, and further water was released into the bowl in ratio to the amount that the chickens drank. Enough said – he'd never quite sorted out exactly how it worked.

He walked over to the pigs and passed the time of day with them, if grunts and snorts can be considered conversation. In reciprocation for attending to the pigs and chickens, he occasionally did chores for the farmer. Already kitted out for such duties, he knocked on the farmhouse kitchen door, and after mutual updates on life he was duly allocated to mucking out the cowshed and stacking bales of hay.

Two hours later, ready for lunch, he showered and changed and feasted on local Cheshire cheese on toast with sliced beef tomatoes and a drizzling of virgin olive oil and Modena balsamic vinegar. This was accompanied by a glass of Real Lavrador red wine, brought back by Amelia from her last holiday in the Algarve. She said it had cost about two euros, but he had to accept that cheap though it may be it was still delicious.

He was seated in his conservatory, listening to a Rhydian Roberts CD. Deliberating on what he now knew, he thought Jenny should start asking some searching questions of Samir. His thoughts centred on how to approach Jenny, as the wrong tack could be devastating.

As usual in these situations, he crunched hot peppermints and paced and pondered, staring unseeing into the garden for some inspiration, not realising the CD had stopped half an hour before. Reaching no conclusion, he collapsed into a chair.

He was in a quandary! He was going to be away for a couple of weeks in May on a consultancy job, in Jeddah, Saudi Arabia, for an international construction company, where the whole structure of human resources was falling apart. Men were quitting right, left and centre, the various projects were way behind schedule, and financial penalties were being incurred. He knew that Jenny had decided to see less of Samir, and that she was going to Florida with an old girlfriend for two weeks and would not be back until the end of May. Things could easily escalate in a few weeks. He would need to speak to Bill Lambert again, and also other contacts.

An hour later he made the call. 'Hi, Bill, about our conversation last week: I am going to be away for a while, but in the meantime I think I can be a little more than hypothetical, but obviously still on a confidential basis. I've got a name you might like to keep tabs on: Samir Khan he lives in Wilmslow, 365 South Canterbury Drive, and works for a firm of accountants in Stockport called Anders-Lybert. You've got my email address and mobile number.'

Lambert was grateful, but knew not to ask further. 'That's great. Just pop me an email if you hear more, and if anything breaks I'll let you know.'

Short and sweet – their long history made obfuscation unnecessary.

Early evening, he called Jenny, and she revealed that she had decided to cool her relationship with Samir and only see him now and then, which as she was going on holiday with a girlfriend to Florida in a couple of weeks' time would not be very often. He, in return, advised his opinion of Samir and his own plans for May, and they agreed to keep in touch if necessary and meet up on Jenny's return from holiday.

Chapter 7

Samir was in a review with his tutor, and it was not going at all well. He had failed his exams the previous year, and in all probability would repeat the process again, as well as having missed a lot of lectures. The accountancy course had outlived its usefulness, and he would be able to let it fade away in a few weeks anyway, to the obvious disappointment of his father, who some years prior had optimistically dreamed of his son as a future Chancellor of the Exchequer. Samir left the tutor's room somewhat stressed. Fortunately it was early evening and he was able to go straight to his martial arts class held in an old brick-built mill that had seen better days in downtown Stockport.

He had first gotten into martial arts at university. He had been athletic at school, mainly cross-country running and soccer, where the stamina gained from the demands of cross-country made him a natural for midfield. At university he became mates with Brian Johnson and Will Foster. Brian was the tallest and by far the heaviest, and his fearless aggression also made him a natural choice in the pack of the second eleven Rugby Union squad. During their sparring at kick-boxing,

Will and Samir were saved from injury only by both being particularly fast and agile.

Back home Samir advised his father of his intention to quit his accountancy studies; the look on his father's face said it all.

Mansoor adored his son, and despite being a very shrewd businessman, "there are none as blind as those who will not see". He had wondered for some time what exactly Samir did with his time – the boy clearly was not spending that much on his studies, and he only spent the minimum time required to keep his job. One could not party all the time. They had had long discussions about the business, and on occasions Samir had assisted Mansoor in periodic tasks of a financial nature, but when the subject of joining his father in working in the business had been brought up, he had always managed to avoid being committed, much to Mansoor's further disappointment.

Samir was saved from any debate on the subject when the phone rang, and like many busy men, fathers or not, the questioning thoughts drifted out of his mind as he concentrated on the next deal.

It was Friday 25th May, and the group was in yet another meeting with Hussein and the imam. Ibrahim Abelgadar had returned to London, and Hussein seemed to be in total charge, if still not talking much.

The imam was the communicator. 'Samir, the report about your visit to the British Museum was excellent, and your comments about Islam's Sacred Shrine confirm that you are a worthy choice for the mission. Ali and Abdullah, your work in assisting me has been exemplary, and together you will make a good team. Your place in heaven is assured, and Allah is pleased to have such faithful soldiers.'

This speech carried on in similar vein under the watchful eye of Hussein, who remained as impassive as a piece of granite, save for the fiery embers burning from those coal-black eyes.

And then it happened: there was a commotion outside, and raised voices, then a man screaming as the door burst open. 'Imam, imam, please help me. They have my daughter, they have my daughter. She is defiled! Oh Allah, be praised. Please help!'

The man was distraught and hysterical, and was only calmed by a sharp slap from Hussein, whereupon he collapsed, weeping, in a heap on the floor.

The imam regained control. ''Water, bring water immediately.'

Khaled Reza's story was heart-wrenching but not unique in 2012 in Greater Manchester. There had been convictions of Asian gangs in several towns for grooming vulnerable young white girls for sex and passing them around, even taking them to other towns. The difference here was this girl was Muslim. Khaled had married a white girl, Sandra, who had been killed in a road accident twelve months before, aged thirty-three when their daughter Raisa was twelve years old. Raisa had the complexion and looks of her mother. Khaled was a factory cleaner, and had been made redundant six months ago. Social services, in their wisdom, had deemed him unable to look after Raisa, and put her in a children's home. He had found out about the abuse an hour earlier whilst visiting the home. Raisa was subdued and crying, and eventually it all came pouring out. The imam barked instructions for the well-being of Khaled and Raisa, and the immediate calling of the police.

Hussein, ever keeping his own counsel, had other ideas. He was not going to be around Manchester for very much longer, and knew Raisa could not wait while the police and authorities moved at snail's pace to administer their pathetic form of justice. Considering his brutal existence, Hussein obeyed a very strict moral code (albeit only as interpreted by himself) direct from the Koran: for he was about to unleash the Sword of Allah.

Hussein called the group together. 'It is time for you to be tested in action. You are now on a mission from Allah! Samir, my sources tell me you are trained in martial arts, and Abdullah, you help your father in his *halal* butcher's shop where killing animals and the sight of blood is commonplace, so you can use a knife. Ali, you are a bouncer at a Manchester nightclub in the evenings?'

The three nodded in unison.

'What is our mission?' asked Ali.

'Vengeance by the Sword of Allah,' decreed Hussein, his black eyes burning.

They left immediately; knowing their target, for Khaled had tearfully related the full story of rooms above a takeaway where the girls were taken. It was in an old terraced street reminiscent of the television soap opera Coronation Street, not far away from Salford Quays and Media City in miles, but light years away in reality. The cobbled back entry was dirty and dingy, with overflowing dustbins, just like they had been for over a hundred years. The group donned black cloaks, and red and white *keffiyeh* covered their faces. There were half a dozen men smoking and chatting in the back yard as the trio burst through the tall back gate. The men were bold at first, and drew weapons. One lunged at Samir with a bottle, but he was too quick and a karate kick left his assailant writhing in agony, holding his shattered knee. The three men in front of Hussein were no match for the Sword of Allah as he slashed right and left with his knife, before moving on into the kitchen. Abdullah worked his knife with consummate skill, slicing arms and thighs to the bone. The remaining men were beginning to flee under the relentless onslaught of Ali, Abdullah and Samir, the last two staggering like drunks as Ali grasped them in a bear hug and smashed heads together like toys. The three were now bloodied and indeed still in battle, but nothing could have prepared them for the carnage they found on entering the kitchen, where Hussein was slicing a man's throat from ear to ear. The greasy white tiles were now splattered with blood, which dripped into prepared food on the steel tables. The group watched in amazement as Hussein dropped the now dead man, rinsed and wiped his knife. It had lasted fifteen minutes. Anyone in the house had now fled, and police sirens could be heard in the distance.

Hussein gave orders. 'Quick we must move fast!'

They followed the back alleyway in the opposite direction and continued through other alleyways, crossing several small streets and making two or three right and left turns to confuse anyone brave enough to have followed them.

Hussein again, 'Remove your *keffiyeh* and cloaks. Abdullah, give me your knife.' With that he wrapped it and his own in the cloaks and stuffed everything into a dustbin. 'We must split up to return to the mosque. Samir, you walk with me and remember walk slowly and keep talking about something trivial.'

Back at the mosque Hussein appeared as calm as any of them could recall, as if somehow his demons had been exorcised at least temporarily. He did not seem to fear being under suspicion for the deeds they had just committed.

'You performed well, all of you, in the service of Allah. Do not speak of today even between yourselves. I am proud to lead you in your real mission, but you must now vanish and tell no one. If you have a beard, shave it off; if you do not, grow one. I will be in touch about a safe house soon.'

Chapter 8

The vigilante slaughter and maiming of a number of Asian men in the back of a takeaway shop in Manchester was not yet national news after several days of a media blackout, but the newshounds could not be held at bay much longer.

It was Thursday 31st May, and Inspector Bill Lambert was in an emergency meeting of the GMP Counter Terrorism Unit (CTU). The unit established in April 2007, and was part of the main strand of the ACPO (Association of Chief Police Officers) and Home Office plans to tackle the terrorist threat in the UK. Also present at the meeting were two Counter Terrorism Security Advisers (CTSAs). The meeting was chaired by Assistant Chief Constable Henry Partridge, who was not happy. 'Bill, you got some information from a source about a week ago. Is there any further news?'

'No nothing as yet. The source is good, but his info is only hearsay at this stage as far I can see, although from what I've heard of this takeaway hit we're dealing with a serious outfit, and if there is a terrorist cell operating out of Manchester with a view to a London target, then that would explain how they could react so fast and effectively. There's loads of Asian low-life practically queuing up for protection right now!'

The Chairman turned to Shug (Shugofta Raman), a female CTSA based in the city centre. 'Shug what's your slant on this?'

Shug gathered herself. 'You're right; there is genuine fear out there. It was extremely fast and brutal – an execution in no uncertain terms – and no one heard them coming. It was all over in minutes and they appear to have just melted away into the night. If anyone saw anything, they sure aren't saying.'

'OK, thanks for that.' The Assistant Chief Constable turned to Malcolm Brampton, the CTSA on his left. 'Mal, what's the view from the airport?'

Mal, a gruff Scot, replied. 'Well, sir, much the same. Most Asians are incredulous at the audacity of the gang who did it, and many people from all ethnic groups are saying the traffickers got what they deserved, while others are expressing the view that people can't take the law into their own hands. As regards the preacher Ibrahim Abelgadar, who has been in UK for the last six months, entering via Heathrow, there is no data to suggest he has left via Manchester Airport.

Certainly not under that name, so we don't know where he is.'

The Assistant Chief Constable muttered something under his breath, and no one was in any doubt that the expletive began with the letter 'f'. 'We don't have a lot to go on right now, do we? I'm supposed to have detailed reports to CPNI and JTAC (Joint Terrorism Analysis Centre, MI5) by five o'clock today. We'll close it there for now, then. Ramp up the pressure on all your contacts and let me know of anything straightaway.'

The Security Service, often known as MI5, was the UK's national security intelligence agency. The Security Service had had a variety of names, most famously MI5, since it was established in 1909. This often led to confusion about what the Service had been called at various points in its history. The Service operated under the statutory authority of the Home Secretary, but it was not part of the Home Office. It was responsible for protecting the UK, its citizens and interests, at home and overseas, against threats to national security. SIS (formerly MI6) was the Secret Intelligence Service, overseas, located at Vauxhall Cross, London. It was responsible to the Foreign Secretary for gathering intelligence outside the UK in support of the government's security, defence, foreign and economic policies. Confusion still reigned by websites being named mi5.gov.uk and mi6.gov.uk respectively.

MI5 had its headquarters at Thames House, a Grade II listed building at the corner of Millbank and Horseferry Road in central London. It overlooked Lambeth Bridge, a few hundred yards south of the Houses of Parliament on the north bank of the Thames. There were seven branches within the Service, each headed by a director. Two departments received a report from GMP that day, Thursday 31st May at four fifty-seven p.m.: CPNI (Centre for the Protection of National Infrastructure reporting to the DDG) and JTAC (Joint Terrorism Analysis Centre reporting directly to the DDG).

It was ten minutes past five in the afternoon, and John Latham, Department Head (JTAC) was gazing at boats motoring up and down the River Thames with bunting flags, practising for the Queen's Jubilee weekend from 2–5 June. He was quite moved with all the pomp and ceremony for the queen, but was beginning to get a bit pomped out what with beacons to be lit across the country, and all this in addition to Olympic flames being carried from town to town. Was it all a cunning plot, he thought, ordered by the shadowy Brussels elite to take people's mind off austerity measures and bank failures – for the summer months at least! One thing he was sure of: the cost would be coming out of his taxes.

He was expecting reports from Manchester about the killings there and any links to London. He'd had the usual nutter email advices about Elvis attacking Parliament and Lord Lucan in Trafalgar Square, and he'd even had three alleged sightings of Osama bin Laden: getting off a boat at Hastings, wearing a kilt in Sauchiehall Street, Glasgow, and standing in a queue at the Tower of London. He was just about to call it a day when in walked Gloria, his ageing PA, dressed in a tweed suit despite the heat of summer and bedecked with her usual grey bun. Her spectacles dangled from a gold chain around her neck, and now past mourning Harold, her husband of thirty years, she attempted to sashay across the office but unfortunately failed as she was still unaccustomed to her new fashionable higher heels.

'I thought you should see these right away, sir, as you've got a meeting in the morning,' she uttered breathlessly, placing two emails on the desk, one being the expected one from Manchester and the other of less import.

'Oh yes, thank you, Gloria,' Latham replied. 'I'll go through it before I leave, in case I need to give anybody advance warning before the meeting tomorrow. See you in the morning, bye.'

It was nine twenty-five in the morning, and John Latham entered the room to chair the meeting.

Present were two intelligence officers from JTAC, one from CPNI, and an intelligence officer from MI6.

Latham spelt out the main items on the agenda: 'The items were originally detailed as London general, Jubilee, as it starts tomorrow, followed by other major events: Wimbledon, Olympics, etc., but now that the media blackout is about to be lifted can we deal with this takeaway massacre in Manchester last week? You've all had a copy of the report from Manchester GMP, which frankly gives us bugger all to go on. What I don't understand is they give us the facts of the massacre but don't seem to have a bloody clue as to who may be responsible, and yet are able to state that a group from Manchester may be planning something in the Capital and it could be the British Museum, but we know jack-shit about it. Ralph, is your agent up there not in touch?'

Ralph (JTAC, IO) was slightly put out by this comment, but there was no trace in his reply. 'Well, guv, as you know in my FYEO' (For Your Eyes Only) 'yesterday, we had information about a possible attack from a cell operating out of Manchester, but routing is direct to me, so how do GMP know about it? My agent, for security reasons, has no contact with GMP, so I can only surmise that there is another party in the frame.'

Jodie, the other JTAC IO, held up her hands and could offer nothing, similarly Marlene from CPNI.

Latham questioned sarcastically to Monty from MI6, 'Don't tell me the FO (Foreign Office) knows more than we do?'

Monty was as brief as only he knew how. 'I have had reports in from all my contacts in the embassies, and also contacts in other far-flung offices and consulates, and they have expressly denied any knowledge of a Manchester faction even remotely potentially involved in a London target. All my office colleagues have been apprised of the incident and are unable to make any comment that would...' He stopped in mid flow.

Latham was a volcano about to erupt with a tirade of foul abuse at the assemblage, and his apoplexy was controlled only by Gloria, who entered the room with coffee and biscuits. Latham's was the only coffee to contain a stiff brandy, Gloria having earlier observed his stress level.

The medicine worked: Latham was a

changed man and almost apologetic. 'OK, now that we've all calmed down...' A team thought-bubble appeared in the air above the table: "We?!" 'Does anyone have the faintest idea why the British Museum? Don't forget the Jubilee celebrations start tomorrow. All potential perpetrators have either been picked up already or if they so much as move a muscle will be nabbed immediately.'

Silence ensued. Monty opened his mouth to speak, but thoughts of self-preservation prevailed. The meeting continued for another hour on other minor alerts in various parts of the Capital, which for the most part had been curtailed or plans were firmly in place should any potential perpetrators make a move.

Latham closed the meeting in sombre fashion. 'Right, everyone, make sure you pull out all the stops. I've had it from the top, and that's the Prime Minister's office at number ten Downing Street, that the news blackout on the Manchester massacre can only be held back until after the Jubilee weekend at midnight Tuesday 5th June. Internet speculation is running wild, and ITN and Sky News won't play ball any longer. There's going to be severe pressure as to why it's been held for this long, but let's hope Number Ten's spin doctors can work up something and keep most people focused on the Jubilee.

Chapter 9

The Gent took a direct British Airways flight from London Heathrow to Jeddah, leaving at 21:30 hours. The flight was comfortable, and he slept most of the six hours thirty minutes, arriving at King Abdulaziz International Airport at 06:20 the following morning. After clearing passport control, a customary search was made of his luggage. *This could take some time*, he thought, as each item of clothing in his first bag was unceremoniously unfolded, and he was becoming alarmed at the intensity of the search when fortunately the next officer along found something of great interest in a package he was searching and his own was passed over. Entering the arrivals hall, he was warmly welcomed by Gus MacDonald, the construction manager, who grabbed one of the cases and led the way from the air-conditioned arrivals hall through the automatic doors leading outside, which was like walking into a furnace. The air burned his throat. He was relieved that Gus had the air-conditioning system turned to as cold as possible in the Toyota Estate for the journey downtown. The company had rented two villas in the Bani Malik district, not far from

the Jeddah Marriott Hotel on the corner of
Palestine Road and King Fahad Street. Gus
and half a dozen other managers had one, and
more engineers were quartered next door.

It was Friday, the day of prayers and the
one day of the week that the men did not have
to work. To a background of calls to prayers
from the local mosque, introductions were
made. To great delight, he produced from his
unsearched suitcase six packs of Danish
bacon, which were seized immediately as it
was time for breakfast. He was lucky: had a
more detailed search been made at the airport,
the bacon would have been confiscated. Later
in the day most of the men drove north out of
the city to Jeddah beach, beyond the creek,
where they could relax and top up their tans
away from the attentions of the patrolling
religious police who would beat people with
bamboo sticks for displaying too much flesh.
Some of the men would swim or snorkel off
the reef, where the colours of the coral and
myriad of fish were an amazing sight to
behold. This left time for Gus to discuss some
of his more pressing issues.

Moving into Gus's office, the Gent was
amazed to see an old fax machine.

'Gus,' he remarked, 'that thing gathering
dust over there must be over twenty years old
by now, surely, and be classed as an antique!

Is it worth much? Does it still work, even?'

'Ye may jest, young man, but I had to use it only last week for correspondence with a construction site in Africa, where although they do have an old computer in the office it had broken down. There is a bit of a story to this. We had three offices in the Kingdom (Saudi Arabia) back then: this one in Jeddah, one in the Capital Riyadh, and another in Al-Khobar over in the East on the Persian Gulf. We could not trust the postal service, so everything had to be sent by courier service. It cost us tens of thousands each year, then one day we got this new whippersnapper young accountant, who explained that the new phase-three fax machines were becoming standard and were reliable. He wanted to buy three of them, at a cost of nearly four thousand pounds each at the time to put one in each office. Took a bit of convincing with corporate Head Office, I can tell you, but ended up saving us thousands over the years.'

The Gent was impressed. 'There's technology for you. Fantastic when it works, eh!'

Gus put the coffee on and they got down to business. Apart from the recruitment problems in general, Gus had a few issues to discuss, not least having two engineers in jail on charges of selling *Sid* (Siddiqui – the meaning in Arabic was *my friend*, an alcoholic spirit often illegally distilled by ex-pat chemists). The Gent offered to approach the Embassy for their assistance in dealing with the legal process of the imprisoned men.

They talked about cash flow and how long it took Head Office to respond to his requests for funds to be transferred. Were they aware of the number of days to reach the local branch in Jeddah after routing through the corporate office? An hour was spent on arranging site visits, at two of which he was to pretend to be an accountant visiting from the corporate office, and could they have a payment now please? The usual reply being, "The Sheik is not in today".

The rest of the trip was devoted to the minutiae of contracts and personnel details in particular. The main conclusions were that the recruitment organisation back in the UK was simply not doing its job, and the remuneration package was not keeping pace with the market. His recommendation would be to stop all payments to the agency forthwith and find a more professional outfit.

One positive aspect of the trip was that evenings were mostly quiet in Jeddah, which gave him time to catch up with his reading. Currently he was halfway through the third book in a twelve-book series by one of his favourite authors, C.S. Forester, about the exploits of Horatio Hornblower, a Royal Navy officer during the Napoleonic era. He was not sure why he had chosen this book; it may have been something to do with the juxtaposition of reading about the sea in the middle of the desert, or even the fact that the author had been born in Cairo, Egypt, the other side of the Red Sea from Jeddah, Saudi Arabia.

With regard to the men in jail, the Embassy was reasonably confident that the court would be convinced that the *Sid* was not being sold commercially but was only for personal use, as the quantities were so small. This meant a much shorter incarceration, most of which had already been served. The chastened men proclaimed to be ever in his debt, and he left Jeddah on a much more positive note than when he had arrived.

After first flying from Manchester by shuttle, Jenny and her childhood friend Anita boarded the Boeing 747-400 jetliner at Gatwick, bound for Orlando, Florida. Both were excited, as neither had been to America before. Flight time was scheduled for nine hours. Flying premium economy in a World Traveller Plus cabin, they enjoyed added extra privacy and relaxation, so after complimentary drinks and a three-course meal, they settled in to watch a film, *Albert Nobbs*, starring Glenn Close as a woman passing as a man in order to work and survive in 19th-century Ireland. The women's choice of clothes for the journey made them almost look like twins: light pastel tee-shirts, skinny jeans and wedge sandals. This allowed them to sleep soundly for a few hours following the film, while the remaining time was spent reading and planning their days ahead.

It was their intention to chill out for a few days and visit the Epcot Centre. They chose Disney's Coronado Springs Resort for proximity to Epcot, and also with an eye on their budget. Located in close proximity to Disney's Hollywood Studios, Disney's Coronado Springs Resort celebrated south-western, Mexican, and Mayan architecture. The rooms were comfortable and had everything they could have needed. An hour in the pool and fitness centre ensured a hearty appetite. They dined on fiery south-western cuisine in the Mayan grill.

Anita had recently ended an abusive long-term relationship, and was coming to terms with putting her life back on track and had confided in some depth to Jenny. Jenny had been deliberately vague about her own situation with Samir, and although she was avoiding the subject for the moment, she was wondering what and how much to say to Anita.

The Epcot theme park icon, Spaceship Earth, looking like a giant golf ball rising high above the horizon, welcomed the women as they walked through the Park's main entrance. Beyond Future World, when entering from the main gate at Epcot theme park, the World Showcase Arena is the first event. World Showcase was a collective of Pavilions that wrapped around the World Showcase Lagoon. Inside the Pavilions were shops, attractions and restaurants representing culture and cuisine of eleven countries. The women focused mainly on Japan, Morocco, and USA. They each rode a Segway Personal Transporter, but after a day and a half, Epcot and the rest of Disney held no further attraction.

Their other destination in Florida was Sarasota, a city of fifty-two thousand on the Gulf of Mexico south of Tampa Bay, made famous by the Ringling Brothers Circus amongst other things. Checking out of the hotel, renting a car was a daunting task, as neither had rented before, never mind driven on the other side of the road. For once the colour of the vehicle did not seem important. Alamo were offering an extra driver for free, and the lady at the check-in desk was extremely helpful and arranged for an assistant to show all that was necessary on the vehicle, to mark up maps, and provide notes to guide them out of Orlando. The I-4 West and I-75 South freeways were a dream after driving in England, and the little air-conditioned Chevrolet Aveo automatic performed without fault, although even with air-conditioning a change of clothes into vests and shorts was required.

Silver Sands on Longboat Key was perfect for the beach. The first morning, after a light breakfast of fruit juice and cereal, they donned bikinis and dedicated time to the sun and the application of factor 15. Anita raised the spectre of Samir, and this time Jenny could not duck the issue.

'You know, of course, that I was seeing a lot of him a month or so ago, and I did mention that things were becoming a bit claustrophobic. Some of the people he has been going about with recently are Muslim, but it's not that in itself, because so is he, but they are... I suppose more zealous and go to prayers every Friday, so of course he has started to go more often as well. But he has become distant, and I don't know who he is anymore. Did I tell you he dragged me all the way to London to check out some special Islamic exhibition at the British Museum? I was able to do my own thing, fortunately, which actually turned out quite interesting in the end, learning more about the Mayan culture – you know we went to Cancun in Mexico on holiday?'

Anita came straight back, 'So that's why we had to stay at that hotel in Orlando with all the Mayan architecture, and have dinner in the Mayan grill!'

'Well, not the only reason, but it did seem a good way of choosing between one hotel and another.'

'Are you still going to keep on seeing him, then? Only I suspect from what you have said that you are definitely going off him.'

Jenny thought the chat had gone better than she could have hoped, without revealing her grave concerns about what Samir may be up to, and notwithstanding her burgeoning feelings for the Gent.

'I suppose I am cooling a bit. Not been seeing much of him at all, actually. Perhaps things have run their course and this holiday gives me the chance to sort out my feelings once and for all.'

Anita was on a roll now. 'What about this older bloke from the golf club, then? You seemed to have a fair bit to say about him last time we met.'

Jenny tried not to blush. 'Oh, he's just a friend, really, who helps me out with my golf. I don't think he's interested in me.'

'Well, that's all right, then,' Anita responded smiling inwardly. 'Shall we have a look round later? We can't lie in the sun all day every day. I'm burning already even with this factor 15.'

Later that day, they found themselves wandering around the shops at Saint Armand's circle on Lido Key. They purchased trinkets, a locally made leather belt and more sun block. In the afternoon they had hoped to have a drink or a late afternoon lunch at Hemingway's Retreat, named after the famous author Ernest Hemingway, but unfortunately they found it had closed. Instead, Venezia proved a good choice for pizza.

The women toured downtown Sarasota and other attractions including the Ringling Brothers Museum, making sure to steer well clear of the notorious Newtown neighbourhood, known as the Courts, which was infamous for the April 2011 murders of two young British tourists, James Cooper and James Kouzaris. They were gunned down by seventeen-year-old Shawn Tyson, who was found guilty of murder. When the men told him they had no cash on them, he told them:

"Well, since you ain't got any money, I got something for your ass" before firing. He was only sixteen at the time.

For something truly unique before leaving, they had been advised to visit the Rod and Reel Pier on Anna Maria Island. It was a small, two-story ramshackle-looking building, bar and bait shop downstairs, and tiny restaurant perched on top. The menu noted that it had been there since 1947. The blackened grouper sandwich was excellent.

Chapter 10

GMP had been working hard on trying to identify the perpetrators of the vengeance attack. Whilst at this point unable to connect him with the Sword of Allah incident, a brief description of Hussein had been obtained and this had eventually been matched up with that of the football gang's assailant. This found its way onto the desk of Chief Inspector Lambert, who delegated it to Detective Maurice Evans for further investigation. As there was always a covert presence in Chinatown, often undertaken by Chinese-speaking detectives, the details of the description were disseminated among them. Three days later a young detective of Chinese ethnicity reported to Evans.

Sammy Wang was second-generation, the son of takeaway shop owners from Stockport with a 2:1 degree in Law from Manchester. He was bright and ambitious, and Evans, old school to the core, felt a little threatened. Wang's written report was flawless, but Evans still felt he had to make sure before he referred up to Lambert.

'OK, Sammy, how sure are you about the

details in this report?' he began.

Sammy replied with a confidence belying his years, 'Very sure, sir. I have known the two informants for two years whilst I have been working the patch, and any information has always been one hundred per cent.'

Evans enquired further, 'And they both say they have seen a man of Hussein's description entering the flat above the restaurant on more than one occasion?'

'Yes, sir, absolutely adamant, sir,' Sammy confirmed.

'Excellent work, well done, lad,' Evans enthused. 'Let me clear this with the boss and we'll be getting round there pronto.'

Evans went in to report to Lambert immediately.

'Think we're onto Hussein, sir,' he said, placing the report on Lambert's desk.

Lambert studied the report for a few minutes before speaking. 'What on earth is he doing in Chinatown?'

Evans, not surprisingly, had not considered such a question.

'You got me there, boss. I've got no idea. Do you want me to get Wang in?'

'No, get a car sorted and I think we'll just get round there. Bring Wang along, though, as we might need a translator.'

The entrance to the flat was down a dingy alley and up a concrete staircase. Rubbish was stored under the stairwell. The door was only answered on the third knock, and with the door slightly ajar all that could be seen was two meat cleavers. A frightened female voice uttered the words, 'What do you want? Go away.'

With the intervention of Sammy Wang, they were allowed access. The occupants were a young Chinese female and an older Chinese woman who could have been the mother or even grandmother. After trying questions in English, it was handed over to Sammy, who confirmed that the women were in fact grandmother and granddaughter. The place was functional, but about as basic as you could get. Lambert gestured to Sammy to carry on, and for what seemed an eternity the two older detectives stood spellbound as Sammy asked questions and the two ladies jabbered answers at a rate of knots. Eventually Sammy said that he had gleaned all that was possible from the two ladies and nothing appeared untoward, and asked whether Lambert wished him to relate it all now or back at the station. Lambert ordered a watch kept on the place and decided to wait until back at the station where at least there were enough chairs to go round.

With all duly seated and supplied with coffee, Lambert ordered Sammy to begin and leave nothing out.

Deferring to Lambert but also keeping Evans on side, he narrated his findings. 'The story is that the flat is the cheapest place they can find to live after the father of the younger woman, son of the older, died a few months ago. They are Chinese, from Hong Kong, but their religion is Muslim. They work in a Chinese *halal* restaurant in Oxford Road, Rusholme, Manchester, which is close enough for them to walk to work. It seems Hussein took something of a shine to the younger woman after meeting her at a mosque one Friday after prayers, and has taken the mantle of protector since they suffered harassment from their boss at the restaurant where they work. He became aware that they were visiting the Chinese consulate in Rusholme in order to get visas to return to Hong Kong, where they have other family members.'

'Well, blow me!' Evans exclaimed. 'I never knew there were Chinese Muslims in Manchester, never mind Chinese *halal* restaurants.'

Lambert interjected, 'You learn something every day, Evans. What we need to know now is what Hussein is up to. 'Sammy Anything on that one?'

'I'm afraid not, sir. They reckon he has gone away and they don't know when, or if, he will come back.'

On that score they finished for the day.

Chapter 11

The Gent had arrived back from his travels on Wednesday 9th May, but Jenny was not due back from her holiday in Florida for a couple weeks. He was at a bit of a loose end. Lily had assured him that all was well with the pigs and chickens, although a couple were not laying too well, which she put it down to the hot weather. He met with the farmer later on and agreed his list of chores to perform in return for Lily's services.

Speaking with Lily made him feel nostalgic and remorseful for what might have been. His own daughter Sam had died aged six after a battle with leukaemia. He had been away at the time, for which his wife Mary had never forgiven him – and that had been the beginning of the end of the marriage. She'd often said he should retire, but it was never that easy. Once committed, they could have you for life, which as a young man in the wrong place at the wrong time could be short. The calls now came infrequently, but the regular pension came in very handy to supplement more lucrative but sporadic contracts. He would ask to meet his recruitment agent and perhaps go to a few arduous networking meetings to procure more boring consultancy assignments. These soul-searching thoughts reminded him that he had not checked his bank statement for a while. He went online, cursing as he struggled to remember his new PIN number, and then again when he had to go back a page to tick a box that he had actually read a message. His pension was in: that was good, but he would need to transfer money from the deposit account to pay a credit card and meet the end-of-month bills. He logged out of the bank and logged into his investments account, which he kept for a rainy day or to provide further pension when necessary. The stock markets were down again, and like many of the disillusioned masses, he wondered whether to cut his losses and cash them in. Further thought was too difficult for now. It was easier to put the kettle on and leave it for another day.

He looked back at his list of chores for something more exciting than banking. The only unusual one was for the following morning. Gilbert the farmer had asked if he could be around to help with the rounding up and loading of a dozen Holstein heifers for auction at Beeston cattle market. Although he'd done it before, it was not a job to relish. Apart from the mud and gore, being trodden on the foot by a cow – albeit not maliciously – was painful, and even a gentle nudge into steel gates left painful bruises.

In the evening he attended a Cheshire Dinner Club disco event, which was most successful. He surprised himself by dancing to seventies and eighties music with Sheila, a golf-playing architect. He offered to take her out on the following Friday.

The following Friday morning, the Gent had to take the Saab to a Kwik Fit garage for an MOT. The car turned out to need two new tyres, but otherwise it passed with flying colours. He was taking Sheila, the architect, out to dinner that evening, so after a light lunch of grilled halloumi cheese and salad, he washed and polished the Saab and then began to think about the Sword of Allah incident. He had not yet heard from Jenny about Samir's parents; he would put off ringing her until the next day.

As befitting an architect, Sheila's home was a most attractive typical Cheshire thatched cottage nestled on the edge of a small village between the A50 and A34. Sheila answered the door still wearing a dressing gown, and left him to be entertained by Tara her Siamese cat. Tara promptly deposited herself on his lap, leaving him to tentatively brush hairs off his Ted Baker light grey slacks. Ten minutes later, Sheila was ready: dressed in a flattering figure-hugging outfit by Christian Dior, offset with a fine gold pendant and matching earrings.

He was out to impress, so they were dining at the Swettenham Arms, a delightful country inn and the only pub in the hard-to-find village of Swettenham. There was one road in and out of the village. Approaching from the north, a shortcut was available but this required driving through a ford, and he did not want to do that in the Saab.

A sophisticated and apparently demure lady, Sheila allowed him to choose her food for her and he ordered the same. The starter was pan-fried hand-dived scallops followed by Cheshire pork fillet, accompanied by a bottle of Montresor Valpollicello 2009. The evening was highly entertaining, and passed far too quickly with Sheila proving an articulate raconteur.

When he had driven her home, he was pleasantly surprised but far from disappointed when kissing him lightly on the cheek she invited him in for a nightcap. Accepting a pure malt whisky, he was flicking through a TV magazine when an apparition emerged from the kitchen clad only in scarlet bra and thong. His blood pressure rose, and by the time she had set down the drinks he was aroused, which she did not fail to notice. There was no sign of the demure lady now as she expertly removed his pants and the scarlet of her underwear was matched by the equally scarlet lips now caressing his erection. Coming up for air, she rode him like a winning jockey at the Grand National Aintree.

Waking the next morning, slightly shocked, he saw she had brought tea in bed, and the smile said it all: it was back to Aintree, but this time he was definitely expected to be the stud, and if her screams of delight were anything to go by, he would be an export. With promises of love and future trysts, he drove home elated and whistling along to Smooth Radio.

He took her out again two days later and then for a day at Chester Races, where they won five hundred pounds and celebrated with a champagne lunch. Later in the day, most of the cash went back to the bookies, but it had been a truly memorable day after which they were virtually inseparable.

Returning home and checking his voice-mail he found that Amelia had left him a message about a house-warming party coincidentally in Chester, on Sunday 20th May, and suggesting that he accompany her.

Although unsure, he called anyway. After her usual cheerful greeting, she asked, 'How was your trip? I hope you've not got tummy problems with all that funny food?'

'Not at all, and I would be delighted to escort you to the party in Chester. I hadn't been in years, until last week when I went with Sheila, the architect lady I have been seeing quite a lot of. We could we make a day of it, walk round the walls, take a boat on the river. What do you say?'

'Great idea, I've never walked round the walls, never mind been on the river... Ooh! Are you going to row, or will we take a punt?'

'I think we'll go with the flow, shall we?' he chuckled.

'Ha, very droll, See you on Sunday, then,' Amelia finished.

She was quite excited, as despite commuting daily for some years to her job in Chester working in an art gallery, she rarely spent time there for leisure purposes. It would be a pleasant and welcome change from her current project, in which she was totally immersed. As she specialised in figurative art, the owners of the gallery had given her the responsibility of organising and planning an exhibition by the famous German artist Willi Kissmer. This was proving quite a task, and taking much longer than expected, but the owners were not as yet alarmed and trusted her judgement. It was not without its problems, though, as some regular clients were becoming impatient. One in particular was frequently turning up on the pretext of checking when the project would be openly advertised and available to be viewed by the public. In fact, she was beginning to suspect he was stalking her.

It was Sunday morning 20th May, the day of the house-warming party in Chester with Amelia. His first job was to wash and polish the Saab in bright sunshine, then after a shower he changed into a polo shirt and jeans. The pleasant five-mile journey through deserted country lanes over to Amelia's only took ten minutes. Amelia looked terrific, answering the door clad in a loose summer dress with her auburn hair tied back by a ladybird clasp. They drove sedately over to Chester, arriving before lunch. Aware of traffic congestion at any time in Chester, they used the park-and-ride facility, opting for Broughton Heath over Chester Zoo as it was less used than during the working week. Alighting in Frodsham Street, they walked a few yards, and then turned right into Eastgate Street, where they climbed the steps onto the old city walls on the right of the Clock.

Proceeding counter-clockwise, the tour of the walls was extremely pleasant, affording panoramic views of the city, the Welsh mountains, and especially the Roodee (Chester Race Course).

'Did you know, Amelia, legend has it that there is still a law on the statute books that it is lawful to kill a Welshman from the city walls after dark.'

'Could I add a few more to the list?'

'Ah! They have to be Welshmen, and the catch is that you can only do it with a longbow!'

They continued past the castle, where the walls overlooked the River Dee, which was the border between England and Wales, and on back to the Clock, finally descending the steps back onto Eastgate Street before walking through the Roman Amphitheatre and gardens down to the Groves, an avenue that fronts the river. The Groves was crowded, obviously a magnet for tourists, with any parking space being taken up by motorbikes, and in pride of place, half a dozen brightly polished scooters straight out of the sixties. In fact, with more than its share of bars and eatery establishments, one could be forgiven for thinking the Groves was a seaside resort. There were a number of companies providing day and evening cruises. The Chester Boat

Company had an option of two large boats, the *Lady Diana* and the *Mark Twain*. The evening cruises offered musical themes including *Mamma Mia* and music from the sixties, seventies, and eighties. Other boating options were small motor boats and rowboats, but with an eye on a weir not far downstream, they settled for a trip on the *Lady Diana*.

Disembarking from the boat afterwards, Amelia volunteered, 'We are here, you know, at the house where the party is. It's one of those back there on the Groves with the long front gardens. It'll be that one with the For Sale sign. I mean, you wouldn't choose to live here, now, would you? They were left it in Dominic's uncle's will, and they're going to take it off the market because when people come along to view they are turned off by all the people. But they'll try again in the autumn.'

The party was pleasant, if predicable, and they caught the last bus to the park-and-ride in good spirits after a good outing.

One day soon after the party, Sheila brought up the subject of the scar on his stomach. He'd previously avoided discussion about it by promising to tell her everything at a later date. It was not a subject he cared to remember, never mind relate in any great detail to anybody else, however fond of them he may have become. As with Jenny, he sketchily revealed the past about his time at Sandhurst and so forth. This was accepted but did nothing to explain the gunshot wound, fragments of shrapnel left in the body, his post-traumatic stress syndrome or what circumstances had brought such injuries about. He was saved by the bell again when her landline rang. Her elderly aunt had died the previous week, and it was her cousin advising on the funeral arrangements. After Sheila replaced the phone, the topic was temporarily forgotten, and he was able to leave without further reference to it.

He was in the habit of phoning Sheila for a chat every morning, but on Friday 18th May there was no answer. The standard computer-generated message left him deflated. He left a message and was sure she would call him back later. He restrained himself from ringing her again that day, but by the evening he could not resist. He tried again but with no luck. Deflation soon became devastation – she had said nothing about going away, and he was sure he had the right number. Was he being played for a fool? He was the strategist the expert human analyst.

The answer came with the dawn of the next

day when the local paper dropped through the letterbox. Collecting it and the detritus of sales literature, he moved into the kitchen to fill the kettle for coffee, and there it was in black and white across the front page: *Lady Architect killed in car crash*. Stunned, he read on:

"Talented architect Sheila Smithers died instantly when overtaking a tractor and trailer on the A34. A fully loaded milk tanker had backed out of a farmyard straight into the path of her Volvo saloon. Paramedics pronounced the 35-year-old female driver dead at the scene. Police have charged a 59-year-old man from Stoke-on-Trent with causing death by dangerous driving."

The paper fell from his grasp and he collapsed in a chair in disbelief, not moving for several minutes. Whilst he had not known her long, the pain and shock was physical. He knew neither her friends nor relatives, so his mourning would be alone and unnoticed. An hour later he finally moved and went off to tend to the pigs and chickens. The funeral would be the following week. Friends and family would wonder who the well-dressed man was, standing at the edge of the churchyard. As the coffin was lowered, he walked silently away, head bowed.

Chapter 12

The next morning he realised he'd had his mobile switched off in an effort to get some sleep after the day before. Switching it back on, there was a text from Bill Lambert: *"There's been an incident in Manchester – could be your man. Do you know anything? News blackout until June 6th, then all will blow."*

Bloody hell! He thought. He'd advised Bill that it would be wise to keep tabs on Samir. As usual, he paced and pondered in his conservatory. *Bloody police spin. What on earth is an "incident" anyway?*

He decided to call Jenny for an update on Samir. She answered her mobile immediately, knowing who it was from the display. 'Hello, how are you? Back from your travels then? How did it go?'

There was no time for niceties. 'Oh, fine excellent thanks. I'll tell you all about it later. There's been some kind of incident in Manchester. Have you seen Samir lately?'

Jenny started to sound nervous, 'No, I've not seen him for over a week now, and he's not responding to calls, texts or emails. Oh, my God! What's happened? What kind of incident?'

He tried to sound reassuring. 'I don't know at this stage, but it must be big, because there's a news blackout until June 6th, so where that leaves the British Museum situation, I haven't a clue. But it's certainly a good job you've been seeing less of him, although at the moment we don't know what it is or whether Samir is involved. Let me see if I can find out and I'll come back to you, otherwise we can talk some more on the 6th.'after he put the phone down, he continued to ponder. If the group had gone missing and Jenny could not get hold of Samir, then he must be involved somehow, he thought, but what was the incident and how was he involved? The Gent was rarely wrong about a person's basic character, and he still didn't have Samir down as a wrong 'un – a bit of a playboy, certainly, but a terrorist? It was now half past two on Monday 4th June, and they had until Wednesday 6th – or more precisely midnight on the 5th. The newshounds would pick it up immediately and

Someone would leak it straightaway. The fifteen-minute news TV channels would start it off as breaking news, the TV breakfast news channels would be getting policemen, politicians and any old pundit out of bed to appear. All radio stations would be onto it: it might even make some morning newspaper editions. He made some calls, but nothing! Apart from one who had merely confirmed the PR-speak in Bill's text? He would have to go back to Bill Lambert, who would certainly know more by now.

The Gent was not part of the police or any recognised organisation or agency of any kind. His was a parallel world of shadowy networks who sometimes – or often not – gave each other snippets of information, and if one had enough snippets and the intellect to process them, one could reach a conclusion infinitely more probable than a mere hunch, as favoured by popular TV sleuths.

Lambert answered his mobile immediately.

'How are things, Bill? I got your text, thanks, but can you bring me up to date? I'm aware that 'whoever' has gone to ground, but are you at liberty to let me know exactly what happened?'

Lambert was cautious. 'I've got be very careful. Your original info appears to be correct re: potential terrorists. Can you let me know where you got it from?'

The Gent was equally guarded. 'Let's just say it came from a girlfriend of said potential perp.'

'Well, from my investigations so far into the young man's lifestyle that could amount to half the rich babes in South Manchester, but fair enough, it's going to be all over the news in a day and a half. It seems a young girl of mixed race supposedly in care got involved with an Asian grooming and trafficking gang operating from a takeaway shop. The father found out and was in bits and burst into the local mosque just as the group were in a motivational session. They immediately set off in vigilante mode, but by all accounts it turned into something more like Genghis Khan. The father's calling it the Sword of Allah, so you had better be prepared for the headlines.'

Thanking Lambert and promising to keep in touch, he then phoned Jenny to let her know what to expect. They agreed to meet later in the day on Wednesday 6th, after checking out the morning news.

It was the major story of the day. As anticipated, the news channels had breaking news feeds whilst other main stories were being delivered, and all the major tabloids had headlines along the lines of '*Sword of Allah strikes in Manchester*'. There were cartoon caricatures featuring Genghis Khan Look-alikes brandishing blood-dripping scimitars. Khaled, the father, was now in demand by all the newshounds, but was being protected by senior Muslim community leaders who were trying to play down the whole scenario. Meanwhile rightist groups were proclaiming that Sharia law had come to town, and vigilante mobs were running amok. The police were of course doing their best in difficult circumstances, but they had nothing to go on, as the group had gone into hiding.

Although they had arranged to meet up later in the day, the Gent was not surprised to receive a call from Jenny at nine thirty that morning, given the air time devoted to the incident and of course the headlines in all newspapers. She was panic-stricken and expecting a knock on the door at any moment as a girlfriend – or at least a known associate – of Samir, one of the Sword of Allah gang, so he invited her over to talk about it and try and make some sense of it all. His attempts to calm her down over the phone had evidently failed, for she arrived half an hour later tearfully distressed, hair a mess and dressed as if to clean the house in jeans and tee-shirt. She immediately collapsed into his arms. He found providing a shoulder to cry on an attractive prospect. Ten minutes and a large brandy later, Jenny was at least more composed and able to speak coherently.

'I just can't believe he's a terrorist. He wouldn't cut someone up, would he?' she sniffed.

'My thoughts entirely,' he agreed. 'Yes, he is involved with them somehow, but there must be something else going on that we don't know about. When I talked to him at Bannerman's I didn't get the impression he was in any way fanatical or zealous – in fact quite the opposite: rather laidback to be honest. Is there any more you can tell me about him and his family?'

Jenny thought for a moment. 'I've never met his parents, and he has no brothers or sisters – well, he's never mentioned any, anyway. Oh, he did say he had an uncle who worked at Harrods in London, if that's any use.'

'Harrods, Did he say what this uncle did at Harrods?'

'I think he said the job was in security.'

'Ah, now that is interesting. I wonder...' His mind was now working overtime, although no rational conclusions were forming. 'Can you think of other relatives or colleagues who could feature in the scenario?'

'No, I'm afraid not. There's no one else that he's talked about that I can remember. Obviously I know his parents live in Wilmslow, not far from his own place, and his father has a business – import and export, in Manchester somewhere. He did mention his work colleagues sometimes, but the names escape me, and while I tried to be interested, conversations about accountancy went right over my head. I only wish I'd paid more attention now.'

'That's all right,' he replied. 'We may have something to go on with the uncle.'

Jenny was calmer now, but quizzical. 'Is all your information coming from this police inspector, or are there others? I don't know much about you, after all.'

He didn't want to lie, but telling his life story didn't seem appropriate. Then again, he didn't want to put her off.

'You know about my consultancy work in human resources, and after university I was at Sandhurst Military College for a few years. That's where I met Bill Lambert the police inspector, and lots of other people, many of whom did not stay in the military but got high -flying jobs elsewhere. The problem with being at Sandhurst is that you could say it's a club – they've got you for life, a bit like the Eagles song from the seventies, *Hotel California.* The end of the last verse goes: *Relax, said the night man. We are programmed to receive, you can check out any time you like, but you can never leave*, so people keep in touch and sometimes you can get information not readily available to all.'

Jenny accepted this but came back sarcastically, 'The mystery man, hey!'

'It's probably more than I know about you,' he replied.

'Touché,' she quipped, wondering where to go from here. 'I'm happy to tell you my life story, warts and all, but perhaps now is not the best time. What do you think we should do about Samir?'

'Yes, I agree. I'll keep on digging; meanwhile it might be a good idea if you spoke to Samir's parents, innocent and concerned like, that you can't get in touch with him and see if they appear to know his whereabouts or if he's been in touch with them. We can share info every day or so.'

'Yes, an excellent idea.'

Jenny left shortly after, feeling much relieved that she was not on her own in this predicament. The Gent was also relieved that she had accepted what he had said. There would be ample time to listen to her life story next time they met.

At seven fifteen that evening the landline rang. 'Harry Farquarson, MI6,' a cultured voice echoed down the line from times long past, and he felt the sands of time roll back and immediately knew he was being inexorably drawn into a situation. There would now be no going back! 'Long time, old boy,' continued Harry. 'I heard you were consulting on human resources, for God's sake. How's Mary, by the way?'

'We're divorced I'm afraid – totally amicable, fortunately. Seems I was away from home too much and I can't quite compete with millionaires. I see more of her sister Amelia, actually.'

'Oh dear, I'm sorry to hear about that. Thing is, I've been meaning to call you because we have been aware for a while now about an Islamic cleric in the country, name of Ibrahim Abelgadar, doing his stuff in London and visiting Manchester. I'm sure you've seen the papers today: Sword of Allah, etc. I've just come from a meeting where Monty, our liaison man with MI5, tells us they received info from GMP on 1st June about a cell operating out of Manchester and also the takeaway hit, but at the time Monty was unaware of this preacher and he wasn't mentioned in the report, so he couldn't comment at that meeting. So in a nutshell, can you give me any intelligence on the situation?'

The Gent had a sinking feeling of déjà vu. 'By sheer coincidence, I do have a lead on this, but need to consolidate before committing further. Although it's a strong lead, it is still only an assumption that the cell is the same outfit that carried out the hit on the takeaway.'

Harry was straight back, 'Good God! If it is two groups then we have got a job and a half on our hands. Well, get back as soon as you can. Your instincts were always spot-on in the old days.'

The Gent was now in possession of a fair bit of intelligence from a variety of sources, none of which was conclusive proof, but where was the group holed up? It certainly didn't look good for them, and did Samir's uncle have a part to play? He pondered for a while over a Bombay Sapphire gin and tonic and decided he needed to have another chat with Bill Lambert. Bill's line was engaged but came back ten minutes later and agreed to meet up at the Forest View Golf Club the next day.

There was no time for a round of golf on this occasion, and he came straight to the point. 'They've tracked me down, Bill. I got a call from MI6 last night from someone I haven't spoken to in years.'

'Don't sound so surprised. It's not difficult – once they've have you, that is it especially if you're on a pension. They just trace you through your bank account; you of all people should know that.'

'Yeah, I know, favours for favours. Anyway, it seems that they know about a preacher who entered the country some time ago spending most of his time in London, but he has also visited Manchester whipping up trouble, but MI5 didn't appear to know about him.'

Lambert was apologetic. 'Yes, the report GMP sent down to MI5 didn't mention the preacher. There could be too many cooks here and no one seems to have the total picture. As for us, we're starting to get some names of people who have not been seen around for a while, but as yet uncorroborated. Even when we do, we still don't know where they have gone, although my guess would be to London.'

'That would be my guess too, but they are bound to make a mistake at some point. Let's hope it's before they get involved in any further action.'

They parted company on that sombre note.

Chapter 13

After leaving the mosque on that fateful day, the group did exactly as bidden by Hussein, preparing their disguises and making up cover stories about their impending absence to spin to their families. They were to lie low for a week to avoid suspicion, as they would if they had disappeared immediately following the incident.

On Bank Holiday Monday, 4th June, when there would be more travellers, the group received instructions from Hussein to go separately to Manchester Piccadilly station and purchase single tickets on a train bound for London Euston. They were to travel in separate carriages, and they would be tracked on the journey. On arrival they would meet outside Burger King, but were not converse. Hussein would be in contact. He had been unable to explain why there had been no media coverage as yet, but the fact that none had been visited by the police was positive. It was raining, dark and cold on arrival at Euston, a thoroughly miserable night. The summer of 2012 would go down as one of the worst on record.

When they were assembled outside Burger King, Hussein materialised out of nowhere. 'Follow me,' he ordered as he walked briskly down the escalator and into the Tube station. They travelled on the Northern line to London Bridge, turning right out of the tube station. It was still raining. Walking a short distance and turning left into St Thomas Street, they carried on, passing Guy's Hospital on the right. On the left was the new Shard building, still a construction site. The road was closed to traffic and all the left side of the street appeared to be under construction work of some kind. It was a dark scary walk past old railway arches, which in years gone by used to house mysterious businesses: Greek import and export, metal tool parts and other small-time operations. They peered down badly lit streets, disappearing for a quarter mile or so under black railway arches. Where the A200 St Thomas Street became Crucifix Lane, Hussein led the trio right into Bermondsey Street, a narrow one-way street going from Long Lane at one end to St Thomas Street at the other. The only exchange during this time had been when Ali had asked if they were going to the safe house, and a muttered 'yes' had spluttered from the grim visage of Hussein.

Street names evoked the history of the area: Vinegar Yard, Tanner Street, and Leathermarket Street. They arrived at Long

Lane and somewhere in that area they at last reached the safe house. There appeared to be half a dozen men inside, and if all were staying it meant sharing rooms and spending the night in sleeping bags. For Samir this would not be comfortable, and this merely added to his stress level. The lounge was bare except for an old table and a few straight-backed chairs, and was decorated in decades-old woodchip wallpaper. Introductions were made but quickly forgotten. Someone brought a tray with mugs of sweet tea and shortbread biscuits, which were gratefully received as no one had eaten much throughout the day.

Nothing more of consequence was said that night, although Ali made the point that he would have expected the house to be in an area with a larger Pakistani concentration. Hussein did not stay, but gave instructions that they were not to venture outside without permission. It was obvious that two of the men were minders, but at least the sleeping bags were clean.

The trio woke the next morning stiff and with headaches after a less than restful night. Spending the night in a sleeping bag on the floor was not all it was cracked up to be. They breakfasted on best-value supermarket cornflakes and were drinking coffee in the lounge when raised voices and several screams could be heard from the rear bedroom. A frightened-looking youth with a bloodied face emerged, accompanied by the loud voice of one of the minders.

'Don't mess up again!' he growled at the unfortunate youth.

The youth's task had been to distribute propaganda leaflets to various addresses, but some had been thrown away down in an alley. It would appear that even the mildest transgression was rewarded with violence.

In the few days after the slaughter, the trio had acted exactly as instructed and discussed the situation with no one. Khaled Reza, the factory cleaner whose heart-wrenching story had set the Sword of Allah vengeance in motion, had seen the group, including Hussein, storm out of the mosque, but had been sworn to secrecy on pain of death. The police had eyewitness accounts of the incident, but no names or where the vigilantes had come from. With the exception of Khaled, the local community did not know either. With their stories holding up, the trio had been able to come and go, albeit nervously for the time prior to their travel to Bermondsey. Upon arrival at the safe house, mobiles had been disposed of and for all intents and purposes they would remain prisoners under the watchful eye of Hussein and other minders until the main event.

What no one could understand was the media blackout. On the morning of Friday 6th June, Hussein threw several newspapers onto the table: their shock was palpable as the headline *Sword of Allah* stared out from the tabloids. They were now fugitives! Outlaws! None of the trio had been in communication with anyone about the incident, with one exception: Samir had texted someone before their mobiles had been confiscated on arrival at the safe house.

It had been well over a week since the group had been quartered in the safe house, and they were all going stir-crazy. The only trips out had all been in the company of minders and only for exercise or to the local supermarket.

It was Friday 15th June, and a treat was in store: Ibrahim Abelgadar was preaching at a mosque not far from Stockwell Tube station. As excitement went, it was marginally better than being stuck in the safe house, though the journey to Stockwell did not feature on any tourist plans. The road from Bermondsey Street to Borough Tube station, Long Lane, lived up to its name.

The ranting and raving of Ibrahim Abelgadar was familiar, with the West being to blame for the ills of the world, but it could be argued that this was exciting after being incarcerated in the safe house. After the speech they were ushered into a back room by Hussein, where Ibrahim was waiting. He greeted them like long-lost brothers, and assured them of their impending martyr status, building up the mood with his accomplished oratory. It was difficult not to feel heroic after such eloquence, although, Samir thought, Ibrahim seemed even more dangerous and mad than previously.

Celebrations were in order, and on the way back they feasted on sharwarma from a street takeaway.

Back at the safe house whilst sat around drinking coffee Samir tried to engage Hussein in conversation.

'Say, Hussein, that was a great speech today, but when do we get to know more about the plan?'

The piercing black eyes conveyed more than the brusque retort, 'You will know in good time. Soldiers of Allah must wait.'

Samir tried again. 'Aw, come on, man, we've been stuck here for ever.'

An iron fist smacked him twice round the head. He fell off the chair to the floor with his ears ringing, then clambered warily back up onto his chair, feeling faint. *Bad move,* he thought as Hussein turned and stormed out of the room.

Ali voiced his concern. 'You OK, mate? The guy's a nutter!'

'My own fault, I guess. We've known that all along. I'll just keep schtum in future.'

The rest of the day was passed reading papers.

Chapter 14

Jenny was meeting Anita for lunch later. They had not been in touch since returning from Florida, and had much to catch up on. But it was still only ten thirty, so she phoned Samir's parents again. She'd had no success after several previous attempts; it was possible they were away on holiday. This time she was in luck: they had been away on a short city break to Venice, and they agreed for her to visit the following day. She freshened up and changed into fawn cut-off slacks with black high-heeled shoes and leather jacket over a pure white top.

She took the train to Manchester. From there she walked the quarter mile to Harvey Nichols department store, and was in the second floor brasserie restaurant overlooking Exchange Square near to the Cathedral in a few minutes. Anita, jacket off, was receiving admiring glances from lunching males, dressed as she was in a tight low-cut pink tee-shirt and short black skirt. She was already part way down a fruity-looking cocktail complete with umbrella; Jenny settled for a dry white wine. The place was full, and some lunching ladies had strategically folded and placed jackets over their chairs in an obvious display of the 'right' labels. Studying the menu, Anita went straight for the jugular, 'How's your Good Samaritan gent, then. Is he good in bed?'

Blushing, Jenny replied, 'Hey, I've only seen him once since our holiday and that wasn't really a date, I've not officially dumped Samir yet, because I can't get hold of him, although I am going round to his parents' house tomorrow to see if they know where he is or why he is not returning my calls.'

Anita looked at her witheringly. 'It seems like you're dithering. If your mind's made up does it matter if you can't reach him? If you don't look like you're interested, someone else will snap up your new man...'

'I have been quite busy with a few things as well as Samir. As you know, my granny has just gone into a care home with Alzheimer's, so my mum needs more support.'

Anita was sympathetic now. 'Oh, I am sorry. I had no idea.' She paused. 'What's the situation work -wise? I thought you were doing well at that solicitor's in Stockport.'

'Oh, yes, I had an annual review the other day. You know I've been working in the conveyancing department? Well, they want me to head up the team when my boss leaves next month.'

Anita was impressed. 'That's great! Will you get a big salary increase?'

'Yes, of course, but it also means I get to look after the celebrities.'

The conversation ended as the waitress arrived to take the order. Anita chose linguine with crab and Jenny a chicken caesar salad.

Jenny spent the journey home wondering how to approach Aisha and Mansoor Khan, Samir's parents, when she visited the next day.

Jenny parked her red Ford Focus car in the driveway of the Khan household and made her way tentatively to the door. She had dressed plainly in a white blouse and jeans. Her finger never quite made the bell as Aisha opened it, in a loose-fitting floral dress, obviously expecting her and looking a little worried.

'Please come in, dear,' she said, leading the way through a bright spacious hall into a square lounge with a view overlooking fields. Mansoor entered at that moment from the kitchen and they exchanged greetings and shook hands. Once seated, the atmosphere was strained as Aisha offered tea or coffee, which Jenny declined.

Mansoor drew his old-fashioned brown cardigan around his shoulders as though feeling cold. He opened the conversation. 'Samir has mentioned you, Jenny, so how can we help you today?'

Cautiously Jenny said, 'It's that I haven't been able to get hold of him for some time now, and I wondered if there was someone else or whether he had gone away.'

Mansoor was honest. 'We know that Samir has, shall we say, a reputation, but we are not aware of anyone serious, and we are not so naïve not to realise that he is not the most diligent when it comes to his work or his studies, but he does seem to be taking this Islamic research seriously, for the moment at least. In fact, he is away in London for two weeks right now for that purpose, along with catching up with old friends from his university days. He said also that he would visit his uncle Sulamain, with whom he lodged initially while studying business at the University of London, Birkbeck College.'

'Have you been in contact recently?'

Aisha looked irritated and cut in. 'Jenny,

121

he is a grown man and does not speak to us every day. I'm sure he will contact you in his own time. Now, if there is anything else?'

Jenny did not want to alarm them. 'No. Thank you for seeing me. If he contacts you, would you just let him know that I was concerned, that's all.'

With that Aisha rose and the meeting was over.

Jenny drove home contemplating. The story was no more convincing than what Samir had told her, but the uncle featured again. She wondered what the Gent would make of it all.

She phoned him later in the day. It seemed to ring for ever, but eventually he answered. 'Are you alright? You sound a bit strange,' Jenny asked with concern.

'No, no, I'm fine,' he answered slowly. 'Someone I knew was killed in a car crash, and I was just thinking about it when you phoned, that's all. Did you manage to talk to Samir's parents?'

'Yes,' Jenny replied. 'Is this a bad time? I could call round tomorrow if that would be better.'

'No, no, I'm fine. What about lunchtime

then?' he said, sounding better.

'OK, see you later,' Jenny ended.

Feeling less depressed at the prospect of seeing Jenny for lunch, the Gent prepared a simple ploughman's lunch with pork pie, Cheshire cheese and pickle, and all purchased fresh from the local village shop that morning. She arrived at ten minutes to one, fashionably dressed, wearing Ugg boots despite it being summer time, which on many women he would have found unbecoming but on Jenny were flattering.

'A glass of dry white wine?' he offered.

'Is the Pope a Catholic?' she countered.

The lunch, though plain, was excellent. Not a scrap was left, and the bottle was empty. He felt human again. Jenny had been cautious throughout lunch and had not mentioned his mystery GMP inspector friend, and she was about to ask when he spoke first.

'Tell me about Samir's parents. Were they open about his whereabouts, or trying to cover up?'

Jenny thought for moment. 'Actually, it all sounds hunky-dory unless you know the background. The story is more or less as he told me, but I did find out he went to Birkbeck College, London, and get this: he lodged with his uncle for a time. He is currently in London for a few weeks doing Islamic research and catching up with old college mates, and of course visiting the uncle. As soon as I mentioned I could not get hold of him, their reaction was he was a grown man and the inference was that I had been dumped.'

'Umm, well.' The Gent's receptors were buzzing. 'The uncle factor again. I think you're well out of this. My instinct is they've gone to ground and it appears no one knows who or where they are.'

'I can you tell you know more than you're letting on. Who are you in contact with?'

'I did mention the inspector from GMP, and another from my early days, but I don't actually know anything for certain. I can see a path forming and will work on it some more. I might try and talk to this uncle and perhaps even go down to London again, with Amelia as cover or better still you, only if you felt it appropriate. No expense to you, of course.'

'Oh, I have just been promoted, but hey! A girl doesn't get offers like that every day.'

'Right then, let me work something out and I'll be in touch.'

He waved goodbye, and with a good bone to chew, his mood improved rapidly. Setting up a flip-chart, he drew a number of squares and circles depicting parties involved in the incident and the potential target of the British Museum. This included GMP, MI5, and MI6, the group and himself and Jenny. He eventually came to the conclusion that taking into account what he and Jenny knew between them and what had been gleaned from Samir before the trio had gone into hiding, they probably had more hard knowledge than the various authorities. They became a circle in the middle of the page with information feeding in. Then of course there was the uncle. Was he just close to Samir or was there more? He would have to find out.

Chapter 15

The Gent rang Harrods and asked for Sulamain Khan. Surprisingly, he was put through and the phone was answered by Sulamain himself. Without introducing himself, he came straight to the point. 'I know something about the Sword of Allah incident.'

The response was terse. 'That's hardly surprising. It's been front-page news all week.'

'I also know you have a nephew Samir, who is currently in London and by all accounts you two are pretty close.'

Sulamain was now all ears. 'OK, who are you and what do you want?'

'Can we meet? I would be happy to come to your office at Harrods.'

Sulamain was business-like. 'OK, the day after tomorrow, one thirty. Go to the Mezzah Lounge on the fourth floor. It is usually quieter there at that time. Make yourself known to the maître d' and I'll come and join you.'

He was about to say thank you but the line was already dead.

The next morning he and Jenny were to travel to London together. She took a local train from Stockport to Crewe and changed to platform one, where she found him passing the time of day with the local Conservative MP for Crewe and Nantwich, Edward Timpson, whose family was famed for the shoe repair and key-cutting empire.

The town of Crewe was perhaps best known as a large railway junction, and was for many years a major railway engineering facility for manufacturing and overhauling locomotives, but now much reduced in size. From 1946 until 2002 it was also the home of Rolls Royce motor car production. The Pyms Lane factory on the west of the town now produced Bentley motor cars exclusively. Crewe was not formally planned out until 1843 by Joseph Locke to consolidate the 'railway colony' that had grown up since around 1840-41 in the area near to the railway junction station opened in 1837. Crewe was thus named after the railway station rather than the other way round. The town had still not gotten over the loss of Rolls Royce and the British Rail Engineering works. After passing the time of day with Edward Timpson, he introduced Jenny as a colleague and they boarded the train, leaving the MP to concentrate on his parliamentary papers at the other end of the carriage.

During the journey he advised her of his conversation with Sulamain the previous evening.

They checked in at the Imperial Hotel in Russell Square, where they were greeted warmly by the assistant manager, who, remembering him from previous visits asked, 'How are things in Cheshire, sir? And what are we up to this time, sir?'

'Oh, this and that, probably shopping, I should think. My associate Jenny here has always wanted to visit Harrods.'

The assistant manager's face was inscrutable as he handed over the keys for two rooms next door to each other on the third floor.

On the evening of 6th June, Samir's father Mansoor arrived home from work. Aisha immediately asked, 'Have you seen the news about this killing in a takeaway shop in Manchester?'

'Yes, of course I have. It's not that far away from the factory, and there was lots of talk about some kind of attack last week, but no one knows who it was or where they came from at this stage. I'm still not getting much work done in the factory what with everyone gossiping about it. Some of them said they would have done the same if it had been their child, but there is a large police presence in the area. I can tell you this, though: it should keep my factory from being burgled again.'

Aisha said, 'You'd have thought Samir would have mentioned it.'

'Well, we haven't seen him, have we? I asked on the phone but he didn't know any more than me. We can ask him again if he rings at the weekend.'

The matter was discussed several times over the next week or so. They did not hear from Samir, but that was not in itself unusual.

On Monday 18th June at two thirty in the afternoon, Mansoor was in a meeting in his office, discussing delivery timetables with the rep from his largest supplier when the telephone rang. It was his secretary; his wife was on the line and could she have a word? He was grumpy. She had been interrupting his day a lot recently.

'Just say I'm tied up. I will be bringing the samples home this evening.'

'I've tried, but she's in a bit of a state. There's something about Samir and the police.'

He apologised to the rep. 'Yes, dear, what's the matter?'

Aisha sounded frantic. 'I've just had a call from Anders-Lybert. The police have been looking for Samir and he didn't turn up there for work this morning.'

'Did the police say what it was about?'

'The lady from Anders-Lybert said it was routine. I've tried Samir's mobile again and it's not working,' Aisha responded.

'OK, I'll get away as soon as.' Mansoor rang off.

He rushed through the rest of the meeting and left for home, his mind in turmoil trying to figure out what the police could be after.

Mansoor had been in the house only five minutes when a dark Ford Mondeo saloon pulled onto the drive: It did not take Einstein to guess who they were. Mansoor was not totally devout – he finished pouring his whisky and gulped it down in one go as Aisha led the pair into the lounge, offering seats and coffee.

Refusing coffee Detective Inspector Bill

Lambert introduced himself and his colleague Detective Sergeant Maurice Evans.

He came straight to the point. 'Mr. and Mrs. Khan, we're investigating a recent incident at a takeaway shop in Cheetham Hill; I'm sure you've seen the papers. Since then we have been round all the mosques in the area. No one is saying anything, but we are checking up on anyone who may not have been seen around for a while. I'm sure you can appreciate that this can include a number of people and for a variety of reasons, but we have to try and eliminate them all and it does take time. Many just forget to let people know they've gone to Ibiza or whatever. It seems that your son Samir hasn't been seen around for a couple of weeks and failed to turn up for work this morning. Have you any ideas why?'

Aisha was unable to speak, so Mansoor replied, 'He is in London visiting friends from his college days.'

Lambert was incisive. 'Do you know why he didn't turn up for work today?'

Mansoor's struggle for words just sounded evasive. 'He's a young man; maybe he's found a girl in London.'

Evans cut in, 'When's the last time you spoke to your son, Mr. Khan?'

131

'Well, actually, not since he went down to London a couple of weeks ago.'

No more needed to be said. Detective Inspector Lambert and Detective Sergeant Evans rose, and Lambert brought the interview to a close. 'Thank you for your time, Mr. and Mrs. Khan. We'll be in touch.'

After the officers left, Aisha burst into tears and Mansoor reached for the whisky bottle. Consoling each other, they sat in silence, wondering where it had all gone wrong.

In the car back to the station Evans asked, 'What do you reckon then, guv?'

'I think we now have a definite link between my information about a terrorist cell in Manchester and the takeaway incident. In fact, let's have an hour out and take a cruise round East Manchester, get more of a feel for the area these days.'

Heading back north towards the city centre, they picked up the M60 ring road and headed east counter-clockwise. Exiting at junction 24, the Hyde Road brought them to Pottery Lane, which became Alan Turing

Way, named after the famous World War II code-breaker.

Passing through Beswick, Alan Turing Way crossed Ashton New Road. On the right was the Velodrome and on the left were Sport City and the Etihad Stadium, the home of Manchester City Football Club. As a lifelong Manchester United fan, Lambert found it ironic that United now played at Old Trafford on the other side of the city. They were originally founded in 1878 as Newton Heat Locomotive a short distance away from City's Etihad stadium, to where City had moved in 2003 from Maine Road Moss Side, the other side of the city.

With the old gasometers still dominating the skyline, they travelled further west along Hulme Hall Lane, through Miles Platting and eventually reaching Queen's Road. Finally they turned right onto Cheetham Hill Road, their destination. The journey was a poignant experience for Detective Inspector Lambert, having been raised in Crumpsall, the next ward to Cheetham Hill.

After the regenerated areas of what is now often referred to as Eastland's, Cheetham Hill retained the air of times gone by, if no doubt modernised. It had attracted immigrants over the last two hundred years, from Irish escaping the great potato famine, Jews fleeing

133

persecution in Europe, to the Asian influx of the present day. Detective Sergeant Evans was driving, so Lambert could indulge in his nostalgic reverie. The Asian influence had been apparent throughout.

They drove north, into Bury Old Road Prestwich, formerly part of Lancashire, and in a few hundred yards the difference was amazing. The affluence was immediately apparent, with larger detached houses and prestige cars. Prestwich and neighbouring areas formed part of one of the largest Jewish communities in the country. Many moved up the road from Cheetham Hill as they became established and more affluent. The Jewish influence was obvious, and the Jewish Telegraph was housed in a shop a few doors along. On the other side of the road not far away, they passed a mosque, the irony of history not lost on Lambert.

Chapter 16

Amelia was floundering. She had lost impetus in the development of the Willi Kissmer project at the art gallery where she worked in Chester. She had sought advice from Willi's agent, who suggested she visit the Maltrom Gallery in London, where an exhibition of Willi Kissmer's work was due to be opened. A lunch was in the offing, where she would have the opportunity to check out the ideas presented by that gallery and meet and greet the agent and other people in the business. She would need an escort, and she knew just the man. If her memory was correct, he was currently in London on some caper or other...

Russell Square was busy both with locals and tourists. He was watching with amusement as a middle-aged lady struggled to control her lively Jack Russell terrier, which had taken a liking to the trouser leg of a Chinese gentleman of diplomatic bearing, who was strolling through the square with his wife and two children. His children were giggling at the spectacle of father resorting to aiming kicks at the yapping terrier, now drawing attention from other passersby. Rescue came at the hands of a dashing jogger, who scooped up the dog in one swoop and assisted the flustered lady in reattaching the leash. Apologies were made and calm was restored.

He was still smiling a minute later when his mobile rang. The display revealed it was Amelia.

'Good morning, Amelia. How are we today?' he answered.

'I'm wonderful,' she intoned. 'Can I interest you in a lunch, with some culture?'

'Sounds good to me, but you know I'm in London at the moment with Jenny.'

'Oh, but I've got to be at the opening of an exhibition by Willi Kissmer at the Maltrom tomorrow, Tuesday. It will be rather posh and trendy and an intellectual raconteur such as you on my arm would be more than useful.'

'Flattery will get you everywhere. Yes, I'd be delighted. Jenny will be out most of the day, updating her aunt. They're having problems with the granny, who is in a care home. Isn't Kissmer known for figurative work? Ladies with backless dresses and stuff like that?'

'The spiel in the brochure is more flamboyant, but in essence you could say that.'

'I'm staying at the Imperial in Russell Square. Do you want me to reserve you a room, Tuesday and Wednesday?'

'Oh fantastic, you are a gentleman, but don't book me in. I'll only come for the day, and I'll let you know roughly when I will be there. I'll need a wash and brush-up if that's OK. Bye for now.'

Amelia replaced the office landline. It was ten minutes past five, time to be off for the day. She looked up and glanced at the street outside, just as a shadow retreated back into a doorway. *Oh hell!* She thought. *It's him again. He must be stalking me. This can't be a coincidence: twice last week and now again and it's only Monday. Surely the precise opening day of the exhibition can't be that important, or are there other more sinister motives?*

She was stopped in her paranoia by the boss bidding her goodnight, along with other employees. By the time she had chatted and finished packing up, she had forgotten about the incident for the time being.

Amelia arrived in Russell Square mid-morning the next day, and the Gent ordered coffee whilst she freshened up. They caught up with gossip, and she volunteered her concern about her potential stalker, though on the evidence – or rather, lack of it as yet – she only her had intuition to go on. There had been nothing personal.

They arrived at the gallery at ten minutes past one. The lunch was limited to invitees only. They were welcomed by pink champagne, and lunch was a buffet affair served in an upstairs room. After short speeches, they plated up and mingled with the arty in-crowd. Willi Kissmer's agent was a garrulous German with a comical English accent. Most of the other guests appeared knowledgeable, but he was out of his comfort zone and could only murmur and nod wisely at appropriate intervals. Amelia seemed to be gaining confidence by the minute as they wandered around commenting on particular pieces. Normal items appeared to be limited editions priced in excess of £500. He liked the look of a particular piece, only to discover it was an original, priced in excess of £5,000. On reflection he decided he didn't like it quite that much.

At about three o'clock he felt Amelia suddenly freeze beside him. A man, impeccably dressed if somewhat dated, was striding purposefully towards them. In his early sixties, of average height but stocky, with steel grey hair and old-fashioned sideburns, he proffered a hand. Amelia declined.

'Fancy you being here!' he exclaimed in a far too intimate manner.

Ice-cool, Amelia responded, 'Merely research, I can assure you, Mr... Ahem.'

'Oh, I was just passing on my way through London. Flight delayed until tomorrow. Are you and your friend here for long?'

The ice was not for melting. 'My brother is here for a while; I have to be back in Cheshire tonight.'

With not the remotest gesture at the existence of Amelia's escort, the man continued. 'Hope this won't delay the opening in Chester, then?'

'Not at all,' Amelia replied. 'It's still on schedule.'

'Glad to hear it. Nice to meet you, sir, must be off. Bye now.'

With that he strode away in the same purposeful fashion as his arrival. Amelia was pale and trembling. 'That's him, that's him. The man I told you about. Is he stalking me now?'

The Gent was concerned. 'It was rather an odd approach. Is he always like that?'

Before they could talk further, Bertie the agent was back and the details of hosting art projects took over. As often happened with being a stranger looking in on other people's livelihoods, it fell into the *how could it be so complicated,* category. He feigned interest until the two experts had concluded.

Bidding farewell to Bertie, Amelia announced, 'Let's finish up here and go find some coffee before I have to head off for my train.'

They were mostly silent on the walk back to the hotel, but once seated and with coffee there was no preamble to his comment, 'I really think you could have a problem with that man. His whole demeanor was strange, and if you don't put a stop to it he will go further.'

'Oh, my God' Amelia said in alarm. 'What

should I do, then?

'I think you'll have to inform the police, and what does your boss have to say about it? Is there CCTV coverage of the street?'

'My boss just thinks I am imagining it all. The man seems to know where to stand just out of range of the CCTV... do you really think the police will take it seriously without something personal and more concrete?'

'You will at least have it on record,' he advised.

'Yes, you're right,' she agreed. 'I'll do it first thing tomorrow.'

With little time left and in view of her still-anxious state, he ordered a taxi to take her to Euston station.

'Call me if anything at all happens,' he said reassuringly as he waved goodbye from the entrance of the Imperial. He watched with a sense of foreboding as the black cab gingerly made its way round the central fountain and out through the archway into the London traffic.

Chapter 17

Jenny was enjoying her stay at the Imperial Hotel, Russell Square. The previous afternoon they'd put off another visit to the British Museum, opting to visit Austin/Desmond Fine Art Events, in Pied Bull Yard, Bloomsbury, where figurative paintings by Aturo Bonfanti from the period 1961–1972 were being shown. This was a little highbrow for Jenny and for the Gent too. A little went a long way for them both.

In the evening they dined at Ciao Bella, also in Bloomsbury. Changing into more casual attire, they exited the hotel, turning left along Southampton Row and strolling in pale sunshine before turning left again into Great Ormond Street, location of the world-famous children's hospital. A final left and they were in Lamb's Conduit Street.

The next day over breakfast they decided to chill out for the morning, and at lunchtime Jenny would accompany him to Harrods, where she could shop for an hour or so while he met with Sulamain Khan, Samir's uncle. They rode the Piccadilly Tube line to Knightsbridge, entering Harrods from

Brompton Road. After passing security, which was serious – much more so than the British Museum had been – they agreed to text if he could not find her after two hours had passed. They parted company, with Jenny off to ladies' fashions while he went in search of the Mezzah Lounge.

He explained to the maître d' that he was meeting Sulamain. He accepted the offer of a coffee and was seated in a quiet spot. The waiter brought his coffee and a menu featuring traditional Middle Eastern fare, which he studied pending the arrival of his host. Bored with the menu after fifteen minutes, he moved on to the *Times*. Another quarter of an hour passed. His suspicion now aroused, he beckoned the maître d' over, who was full of apology and strode over to the in-house phone, returning immediately to advise that there had been a problem and someone was on the way down to escort him to Sulamain's office.

Two minutes passed before a small, dapper man appeared who introduced himself as Hopkins in a strong sing-song Welsh accent.

'Follow me and keep close or you could be lost forever in the corridors upstairs.'

Routing back through a lift, they ascended several floors before alighting into a corridor that he assumed led to private offices. The doors had no numbers or descriptions, and he didn't recall a floor number in the lift either. On entering the room, the dapper man asked him to sit while he went to fetch coffee. He returned shortly with coffee in the company of two large men. Neither was Sulamain: one was Chief Inspector Monroe, and the other was Detective Sergeant Patterson, both of the MET. The Gent took of a sip of coffee while trying to figure out what was going on. Deciding an innocent approach was probably best, he waited, hoping Sulamain would walk through the door any second. Silence was no longer an option as Monroe barked, 'Why are you here?'

'I came to meet Sulamain. Is there a problem?'

Monroe's delivery was pure Hollywood: 'You could say that. He was found dead in the car park last night with a knife between his shoulder blades.'

'What, here? In Harrods's own car park?' he exclaimed.

Another fine mess, he thought as he tried in vain to come up with a suitable riposte. He held his hands up and was about to speak, but Monroe was in first.

'What did you want to see Mr Khan about?'

Whatever he said, he knew he would be digging a hole. 'Well, I've met his nephew and wanted to have a chat about his whereabouts. He's been away from home for a while. No one knows where he is and his mobile isn't working.'

Monroe was expecting rather more. 'Is that it? Is that the best you can come up with? How old is this nephew?'

'Twenty-eight, I think.'

Monroe was now enjoying himself. 'Twenty-eight, you hear that, Patterson? This Mr Clever Dick expects us to believe he came all the way down here from up North just to have a chat to a twenty-eight-year-old bloke's uncle because he hasn't been seen for a bit. Very neighbourly, I should say, wouldn't you Patterson?' Patterson opened his mouth to agree but was too late.

'You got no phones up North then?' Monroe barked.

He would have to put an end to this quickly before it became farcical. The last thing he needed was to make enemies of the two Met policemen.

'Look, there is a lot more to this than appears...' Before he could continue Monroe interrupted.

'You can bloody well say that again, right, Patterson?'

'Yes, sir,' Patterson duly responded.

'If I could phone a friend...'

Monroe was in stitches now, but it gave Patterson the chance to get in. His quick-fire response was, 'Thinks he's on the telly now, sir. *Who wants to be a Millionaire*? That's brilliant, that is.'

The Gent stood up and said with some force, 'His name's Farquarson. Harry Farquarson, MI6.'

The pair stared at each other for a moment as it sunk in.

Monroe was all business now. 'This better not be some kind of joke, or you're straight down to the station.'

'Honestly, no joke. Here's the number.' He wrote it down on the pad provided on the table.

Monroe picked up the phone and punched in the numbers. It was answered promptly, but when he proffered the name he was asked what department. He relayed the information and was advised Middle East affairs. A minute or so later he was through.

'How can I help you, sir?' a female said in a pleasant, cultured accent.

'Mr Harry Farquarson, please,' Monroe asked. There was a stilted pause.

'Are you sure you want Harry Farquarson?' the lady asked.

'Yes, of course I'm sure,' Monroe stressed in agitation. There was a further pause before a red-faced Monroe slammed down the phone. He turned around and commented sarcastically, 'They have no one of that name! What do you think of that, eh? Patterson?'

'Definitely dodgy, I'd say, sir.'

The Gent felt the hole getting even deeper. 'There must be some mistake,' he uttered lamely.

The double act was in full swing now. 'We've heard that a few times, haven't we, sir?' Patterson joked.

'Come on, let's go,' Monroe instructed. 'Maybe we'll get better answers down at the station.'

What on earth is going on? The Gent thought as he was unceremoniously bundled into the back of an unmarked police car. The drive to Kensington police station was silent. Fortunately, whilst they were mightily pissed off with his answers, there was not actually anything yet with which to charge him; he was merely 'being interviewed'. There were about half a dozen people in the waiting area. He was about to text Jenny, who would be getting frantic now, when he observed a grey-haired, smartly dressed black man pacing up and down and murmuring to himself. He appeared gravely disturbed.

'I's praying today, Lord. I's praying today. I's Ready to go now, ready to go.' There was no way of knowing why this man had been brought to Kensington police station, but it appeared clearly evident that the man needed much more support than could be provided by the police or a solicitor.

Keeping his text to the bare minimum, he said that he would be delayed, and advised Jenny to go back to the Imperial Hotel and that he would join her there later. He had been interviewed for half an hour, during which the information he felt he could divulge did not convince Inspector Monroe to release him. He was advised that he would be held whilst further enquiries were made. Time passed interminably, during which the ebb and flow of interviewees maintained pretty much a constant number of those unfortunate enough to be invited to partake in the delights of Kensington police station, together with a few considered more dangerous, who were swiftly despatched to a holding cell.

At some point Detective Sergeant Patterson came in with coffee, and they passed the time of day. The second cup of coffee, received courtesy of Patterson, was distinctly foul. Several hours had passed, and the time was now eight thirty-five, and he was resigned to having to spend the night in a place where time appeared to mean nothing. It just stood still!

Jolted out of solemnity by his mobile, he expected it was Jenny in serious panic.

'Hello, old boy. Sorry about the confusion with names,' chirruped Harry Farquarson. 'I had to change my alias last week after a bit of an incident. The call from your friend Inspector Monroe was recorded, and the techy boys in the back office only check twice a day. Fortunately a request to speak to a recently archived alias raised a red alert and they contacted me immediately. What can I do for you?'

'You can get me out of Kensington bloody police station for a start, where I've been stuck for hours. They know that I know more than I'm saying, and I daren't reveal any more for obvious reasons but I sure as hell don't fancy staying the night. What is your current alias, anyway?'

'Jack Spinner,' Harry replied.

'Jack-the-lad Spinner, sounds true to type if you ask me If Monroe hasn't knocked off early; I'll get him to call you right away. Don't go anywhere.'

'Don't worry, I'll sort him out and I'll catch up with you later this week and you can fill me in about what you have been up to.' With that he was gone.

It took ten minutes to find Monroe and another ten for him to place the call and come back with a result.

Monroe was dutifully respectful. 'I don't know who you really are, but you and your mate, whoever he is, have got some high-level contacts. You're free to go, and I've been instructed to let you have information on the murder of Sulamain Khan as we get it.'

'I am much obliged,' he said, shaking hands as they parted company not exactly best buddies but at least colleagues working for the same cause.

Travelling back to the Imperial driven by Patterson, who was on his way home, they indulged in some mindless conversation, after which the Gent asked, 'What's up with the black man pacing up and down and talking to himself all the time?'

Patterson replied, 'Do you really want to know?'

'I am just curious.'

Patterson was happy to gossip. 'Shouldn't be telling you, but seeing as you're cleared, so to speak: he's over here from Nigeria because his granddaughter disappeared a few weeks ago, just like that. She was staying with relatives, not been in any trouble or anything, always behaved herself. Plain mystery, the old man comes in nearly every day asking about her and do we have any news. Breaks my heart, problem is, though, he says if he finds out who's got her he'll kill the bastards himself with his bare hands.'

'So he's not totally mad, then?'

'No, not at all,' Patterson replied. 'When he says he's ready to go he means he don't care what happens to him!'

'Wow, bit of a story there!'

After a period of silence he dwelt on his own position and wondered whether there was a link between the murder of Sulamain and the disappearance of Samir and the activities of the Manchester group. After a career in the Met, Sulamain was bound to have made some enemies. Other than that and the situation with Samir his main thought throughout the journey was Jenny. He found he was concerned... no, it was much more than that. *Oh damn*, he thought. He had to admit he was falling for her. He thanked Patterson profusely as he waved and made his way across Russell Square.

Jenny was distraught when he arrived back at the hotel. She was sitting in reception sipping coffee, and immediately rushed over when she saw him. Their embrace seemed perfectly natural, even if it lasted slightly too long, going by the stares of one or two other guests, to which they were not totally oblivious. It had a calming effect on both as they sat down.

After a short period of embarrassing silence, Jenny said, 'You know I was so worried about you! I wondered where on earth you could have been all this time. I was just about to ring the police when you walked through the door.'

He began to explain but Jenny continued.

'What did Sulamain have to say? Surely you can't have been talking to him all this time?'

'Slow down, slow down,' he said. 'Let's go get some supper and I'll tell you all about it.'

After ordering large Bombay Sapphire gin and tonics with ice and lime, he began, 'You were right about policemen. When I got to Sulamain's office, there were two Met officers waiting, and when I tried to explain that I wanted to speak to Sulamain about Samir going AWOL, they informed me he'd been found stabbed yesterday.'

Jenny voice went up several octaves. 'Oh, my God! And they thought you had something to do with it?'

'Let's just say my story about travelling to London to speak to a grown man's uncle because he had not been in touch for a few days sounded rather weak in the circumstances.'

'Yes, I suppose from their point of view it would.'

'And when the get-out card of my contact at MI6 did not exist, they fell about laughing and I was carted off to Kensington police station, where they left me to stew for a while.'

Jenny smirked, beginning to see the funny side. 'What happened next?'

'Well, fortunately at MI6 they do actually run checks, twice a day on discarded aliases, so it was picked up. He phoned me back and then after Farquarson's boss explained the alias situation to them they are now offering me any info that comes in.'

'Oh, I forget to tell you,' Jenny offered. 'I've been trying Samir's mobile again, only now there's a message that the number is no longer in use.'

'That sounds ominous.'

After dining on lasagne and salad, they retired to their respective rooms with much to dwell upon.

The next morning the Gent received a call from Monroe that Sulamain's mobile phone had been found. It listed a text from Samir advising that he was being kept under close scrutiny somewhere in Bermondsey and would be in touch soon. Monroe would check if the operator could locate the area where Samir's mobile had last been used. At last, confirmation of a link, but if that text had been seen by the minders, had it sealed the fate of Sulamain? And more to the point, they would now know Samir was an informer, so what fate would befall him? He spent the rest of the morning catching up with e-mail courtesy of the Imperial Hotel's Atrium coffee bar Wi-Fi internet hot-spot, while Jenny visited the Imperial's hair salon. This gave him time to marshal his thoughts together. More information from Monroe would be forthcoming regarding the precise location from where Samir's text had been sent. More about Sulamain's role in the scenario would also be useful, and even more interesting would be what Jack Spinner had to say. No doubt Jack would be in touch soon.

The target occupied his thoughts more than any other. The Jubilee celebrations had passed, and the British Museum currently figured highest as Samir had visited there, but he would have expected the group to have been placed in a safe house in closer proximity rather than south of the river in Bermondsey. Then again, the Olympics were to start in July, but would that be too long a time to keep a group together who were now known to the authorities? The main venue , the Olympic Park located in the east end of London, adjacent to the Stratford City development, was over five miles away and north of the river Thames., whereas the safe house was in Bermondsey, south of the river. To hazard a guess, the less time spent in a vehicle or reliant on public transport for their mission, the better. Was the Manchester group even going to be chosen? Then why bring them down to a safe house in the capital? There seemed to be more questions than answers. He was on a merry-go-round with the British Museum still featuring at each 360° revolution, followed by Bermondsey in the background. He made a decision, that at some point in the not too distant future he would have to visit both.

Chapter 18

The Gent was still mulling things over and waiting for Jenny when he had an idea. Was this about terrorism in general, Al Qaeda-sponsored, or was it to do with any particular sect of Islam? Gus McDonald, the construction manager from Jeddah whom he had visited a few weeks before, was quite knowledgeable about Islam, having been an expat in the Middle East for many years. It was twelve fifteen, and it would be two hours later in Jeddah – siesta time, and too hot for work on many sites. Gus McDonald was most likely to be in his air-conditioned office rather than out on site. The phone was answered on the sixth ring by the male secretary, in perfect English with a slight Pakistani accent. He was put through straightaway.

Gus sounded as if he had been napping.

'It's nice to hear from you. Hope your trip home was OK. Are you reporting back on anything?'

'Actually no, just a small favour, if I may.'

'Of course, fire away.'

'Well, I know you're pretty clued up on Islam and the Middle East. In layman's terms, what would I need to study to gain an understanding about the various sects, etc., in different Middle East countries?'

Gus guffawed. 'How long have you got? It's a life's work for many people, but your starting point needs to be the main schisms, Sunni and Shia, for example. Saudi is mainly Sunni, but of the Wahhabi influence. Qatar, one of the emirate states, has a Sunni majority of Wahhabi influence. Across the Middle East there are states where a minority Sunni group rules and dominates a Shia majority, and vice versa. In Syria Assad's Alawites (Shia) dominate the majority Sunni. Iran is predominantly Shia. You can get a lot of up-to- date stuff from the internet and newspapers, etc. I could go on!' Gus offered.

'No, no, that's very informative. I think there's a lot to learn, but at least I know where to start. Thank you again, and good luck with the project.'

'So long, mate,' Gus replied and the lecture was ended.

Whilst not in great depth, it was enough to refresh his memory. Perhaps a bit of research was needed.

Jenny arrived back at ten past one, looking

like a Hollywood star after being pampered in the salon, with low lights in her blond hair, cut and blow-dried and French-manicured nails.

'How do you fancy an hour in the British Museum this afternoon?' he suggested.

'Great. A girl can't have too much culture, you know.'

'Settled then, a quick sandwich for lunch, then before, we go,' he offered.

An hour later they were in the British Museum.

It was a mistake. He had expected to be able to access the library and browse away for an hour, but an appointment was needed in order to have particular catalogues available. They passed an hour or two wandering around, and had a coffee in the court café. Security did not seem to have improved since the last visit. He was disappointed about his lack of success, and decided that the most useful type of information would be that of a political nature rather than historical/cultural, as in the British Museum. Reflecting on his conversation with Gus McDonald, he decided to research on the internet on various websites and media. He quickly concurred with Gus's opinion that trying to understand the complexities of the Middle East and the

Islamic world was a lifetime's work even for the most gifted scholar. He soon discovered that trying to understand the myriad branches of the main wings of Islam, Sunni and Shia could prove a futile road to go down. One of the most informative overall summaries he came across was an item in Fredrick Forsyth's column in the Daily Express of April 27th April, 2012. Forsyth drew the conclusion that none of the conflicts was a single issue and that the doctrinal differences within Islam are not the West's quarrel.

What did draw his attention were connections to two places featuring in the present conundrum. First, Manchester, Manchester City Football Club moved from Maine Road to the City of Manchester stadium, the centre point of the 2002 Commonwealth games. The club was purchased by Thakshin Sinawatra, the former Prime Minister of Thailand, in 2007. However, this venture was not to succeed, and in 2008 the club was sold to Abu Dhabi United Group, making it one of the best financed in the premier league. With sponsorship from Etihad Airways, the official airline of the United Arab Emirates, the site was now known as the Etihad Stadium. The Abu Dhabi United Group for Development and Investment (ADUG) was a United Arab Emirates (UAE) private equity company owned by Sheikh Mansour Bin Zayed Al

Nahyan, a member of the Abu Dhabi Royal Family and Minister of Presidential Affairs for the UAE. The Group was formed as the investment vehicle for the takeover of Manchester City in 2008. The Etihad Stadium was a stone's throw from the regeneration area of New Islington, and a short distance from Cheetham Hill.

Second, Bermondsey, London, leaving the underground at London Bridge and proceeding through the newly regenerated London Bridge Quarter to Bermondsey, one was confronted by opulence on a grand scale. The brightest and most unmistakable example could only be the 'Shard'. Towering over the South Bank of the Thames, the Shard was the tallest building in Western Europe at thr310 metres high (1016 feet), and consisted of the capital's highest public viewing gallery, offering 360° views of the City of London. His Excellency Sheikh Abdullah Bin Saoud Al Thani, Governor of Qatar Central Bank and Chairman of the Board of Directors of the Shard Funding Limited announced that the official inauguration of Shard Tower in London would be on July 5[th,] 2012. The tower would be inaugurated by His Excellency Sheikh Hamad Bin Jassem Bin Jabor Al Thani, Prime Minister and Minister of Foreign Affairs of the State of Qatar, and Prince Andrew, the Duke of York. A US Congressional report dated June 6th by

Christopher M. Blanchard, a specialist in Middle Eastern affairs, gave invaluable insight into the strategic importance of Qatar in the region: '*their assertive diplomacy has given rise to resentment in some quarters. The power of its government supported by Al Jazeera satellite television station network has made Qatar a key player during the unfolding "Arab Spring", a movement for more democracy in many Arab countries.* The document was twenty-one pages and only served to give him a headache.

Dwelling on all this information for some time brought no firm conclusions. Could there be disgruntled parties plotting revenge for a real or imagined injustice, or was it all pure coincidence? Was it an Al Qaeda-sponsored operation? What exactly was the Shard? Maybe a visit was needed.

He was shaken out of his contemplation by the ringing of his mobile. It was Monroe of the Met.

'Hi, thought I'd let you know, we traced signals from Samir Khan's mobile to a house in Bermondsey. I've just come back from there, and guess what? They did a runner last night. All we found was a body, shot in the back and left in the doorway where he fell, poor bugger. Can't stop, there's another lead coming in. I'll get back to you.'

He was about to offer thanks but the line was already dead, Chief Inspector Monroe was indeed busy. He had wanted to have a chat with Monroe about Sulamain Khan and his role in all this, but he would have to wait until the Met man called back. Jack Spinner hadn't called back yet, either. It was forever a waiting game. Time had gone in a flash. Their train back to Crewe was in an hour.

Chapter 19

Since his visit to Samir's parents, Aisha and Mansoor Khan, on 18th June, Inspector Bill Lambert of GMP and his colleagues had been hard at work checking out Samir and any other persons who had been absent from their homes or work and who had links to the mosque in Cheetham Hill. They had narrowed it down to six people, whose absence was still unexplained. Lambert, of course, already had a tip-off about Samir's potential involvement in a terrorist plot and this was enough for him to link the other two of Samir's friends from MMU, Ali and Abdullah, as connected. The other three absentees would have to be eliminated in due course. Meanwhile, gone missing was one thing but not conclusive of involvement. He knew they were probably in London, but where and what the target was remained unknown. He was being pressured by MI5. It was now Friday 22nd June, four days after his visit to Samir's parents, and he could only give them names and confirm that they were still AWOL.

Other related crimes were now occupying his resources. There had been a spate of copycat vigilante attacks on takeaway shops in other parts of Manchester, but even more alarming was a string of attacks on Asians of any ethnicity, be they Muslim, Hindu, Sikh, Buddhist or whatever. The situation had provided a perfect excuse for far-right groups to attack ethnic minorities and immigrants of any persuasion – in fact; it was the best opportunity for mayhem since the riots of summer 2011. A group of sad characters, originally calling themselves NNI ('Nights of New Islington'), was an attempt to invoke thoughts of the Knights Templar, famous for their ventures in the crusades, before somebody pointed out their obvious lack of attention in school: the name was promptly amended to KNI. New Islington, a regeneration area on the Ashton Canal in Ancoats Manchester, appeared on the eighteen forty Ordnance Survey map. At the last attempted regeneration in the 1970s, it was known as the 'Cardroom Estate', the latter more aesthetic name chosen by the residents along with a projected tram stop giving hope for longevity and prosperity.

It was Monday morning on 25th June at ten thirty, and John Latham, department head of JTAC MI5, was chairing a meeting to update on the Sword of Allah situation.

'OK, guys, we've had a report from GMP identifying a group from Manchester who have gone AWOL, probably in London, but no idea as to where or what they might be targeting. Anyone got anything to contribute?'

Ralph, MI5 IO, was first to raise his hand, 'I have no information coming to me direct from my local agent, but I'll check out the names in this latest GMP report with him.'

Latham didn't actually groan, but his face told a story as Monty from MI6 raised his hand.

'I have expressly requested full updates from colleagues in my department together with contacts in all other departments and do potentially have something to offer at this time.'

Latham was exasperated. 'Monty! Get on with it, man.'

'Yes, sir,' Monty ploughed on. 'I would not normally name names for security reasons, but delegates at this meeting may be familiar with Harry Farquarson, a long-standing MI6 handler. It would seem that because of a recent incident he has had to change his alias to Jack Spinner.'

There were murmurs of confirmation from the meeting attendees as to being aware of

Harry Farquarson.

Monty continued. 'Harry – sorry, Jack – has been in contact with an old colleague who seems to have some knowledge of this cell from Manchester. Jack received a call that this chap was at Kensington police station, and he was being interviewing by the Met after trying to keep an appointment with Sulamain Khan, Head of Security at Harrods. The Met were waiting for him as Mr Khan had been found stabbed to death the night before, and as his story was a bit thin – especially the part where he specifically requested them to contact a name that is currently persona non grata, i.e. Harry Farquarson – Jack was able to arrange for his release, but is yet to meet for further information.'

Latham showed evident surprise. 'Well done, Monty. What do we know about Mr Khan? Why should he end up dead, and is it coincidence or is there a connection?'

Monty responded eagerly, 'We do know he used to be in the Met, sir, but that's all we have at the moment.'

Latham was about to bring the meeting to a close when Jodie, MI5 IO, raised her hand.

'Excuse me, sir, I know Khan is a bit like Smith or Jones, but is there any connection between Sulamain Khan, the dead man, and the Khan mentioned in the GMP report?'

'Well observed, Jodie,' Latham said. 'Can we check that out pronto, and meet again in a couple of days?'

In the safe house, Samir was becoming increasingly concerned. They were virtual prisoners and their mobiles had been confiscated. Had they been destroyed? Had information been lifted from them? Had his uncle received his messages? There was no way of knowing.

Hussein, meanwhile, was satisfied with the situation. He was in touch with other safe houses in the capital, all with minders and cells capable of completing the operation, once it had been decided by Ibrahim Abelgadar. He was aware of the demise of Sulamain Khan, albeit he wasn't personally involved. Samir owed his life to assurances by Hussein that his elimination could spark a panic throughout the safe house, especially with Ali and Abdullah. The minders, mindless thugs both, were effective. Hussein knew they were involved in criminal activities that included travel agencies specialising in *Hajj* tourism at exorbitant rates and trafficking young girls for the sex industry, but the time was not right for his now infamous style of retribution. Abelgadar was a brilliant strategist, and would choose the precise time and target for their particular cause.

It was not often the trio were alone in the safe house and could speak freely. Ali opened the conversation.

'I've had it up to here with all this stuff. Why should we put up with it any longer? We're virtual prisoners, and it doesn't look like we're ever going to be part of anything.'

Samir was subdued. 'Yeah, I agree. I've no idea what is going on.'

Abdullah pitched in on a positive note, 'Come on, guys, we were chosen, right? We never expected it would be easy. It's always a pain when you're just waiting around.'

It was not just the isolation that was affecting Samir: the secrets he held were making him jittery, and without access to a mobile or internet he could not contact his uncle to find out anything, nor could he contact anybody else for help. 'I'm just not sure anymore. Could we really affect opinion without killing lots of people? All we have heard in this place is how to make a bomb, and most of that sounds amateurish. The best comment was from that old bloke the other day that it would just be delivered to us and all we would have to do is plant it and it would be set off remotely. That's fine if you believe all that crap.'

Abdullah again, 'Hey, come on, mate, you're just missing the birds and booze.'

Ali agreed, 'Yeah, let's give it a few more days.'

The group was silenced as three other inmates entered the room, all illegal immigrants. Their English was limited, but what could be determined was that a move to another safe house was being mooted. Samir was heartened to hear this news. It might give him an opportunity to make contact with someone.

Chapter 20

It was Saturday the morning after returning from London. He'd nearly made a pass at Jenny several times whilst they were in London, and it was obvious he would not be rebuffed. The trouble was he was still shocked following the death of Sheila only weeks earlier. He cleared away his breakfast dishes and went to check the chickens. He tried to shoo them all to go outside, but Doris just sat on her perch, a sure sign of something – illness or old age, he thought. He would keep an eye on her and have a word with the farmer.

After the usual chit-chat, and having been given his chores, he broached the question. 'Doris not looking so good today, Gilbert is she laying eggs alright?'

Gilbert seemed downcast. 'She's been like that a day or so now. Maybe she's had enough. She's getting on a bit, and they were rescue hens, as you know.'

'OK, you could well be right. We'll just have to keep an eye on her,' he concurred. The next morning Doris was in a heap at the bottom of her perch, stone-cold dead, and he buried her in the field behind the barn. It wasn't that sad, as she'd had a good couple of years after being rescued – better than being got by the fox.

He checked in with Jenny and offered to take her out that night, but as she started her new job the next morning, they made a date for later in the week. Needing the bathroom, he began whistling and was shocked to catch sight of his face in the mirror, smirking lasciviously.

After lunch and feeling the need for exercise, he pumped up the tyres on his old bike and rode over to Beeston Castle, a former Royal castle in Beeston, in the west of Cheshire. Perched on a rocky sandstone crag 350 feet above the Cheshire Plain, it was built in the 1220s by Ranulf de Blondeville, 6th Earl of Chester, on his return from the Crusades. The castle, now in ruins, is owned by English Heritage and designated a Grade I building. Today the Sealed Knot Society was staging an English Civil War re-enactment event. It was looking more like a draw than a win for the Cavaliers, but it was good fun and the sun looked as though it would burn down all afternoon. The ice cream vendor was busy and happy to chat as he made a large ninety-nine cornet, which was gratefully received by the Gent as he rested his tired legs.

The sight of families with small children made him sad and melancholy at what might have been. He could have blamed Mary, his ex-wife, but that would be unfair. He cast his eye over the Cheshire countryside and could see children riding horses not far away and thought of Sam, who had been riding for six months when she contracted leukaemia. Taking after her mother, she was fine-boned with long, thick, dark hair. He imagined her in the afternoon sunshine, her dark hair flowing in the breeze. An old grey pony called Henry had been her favourite, a gentle beast but with spirit when encouraged. A tousled ginger-haired boy firing a party-popper at him broke the moment and he moved on.

Climbing to the top of the crag, he was afforded one of the most spectacular views of any castle in England, stretching across eight counties from the Pennines in the east to the Welsh mountains in the west. On the way back down he could see the Roundheads and the Cavaliers were packing up and families returning from their walks in the surrounding woodlands and nature trails. It was time to make the ride home.

On Monday morning, 25th June, he realised he had not checked his landline for messages from the day before. That was the trouble with the British Telecom answer message service: you had to remember to pick up the phone unless there was another call, in which case there was a pause in the dial tone. There was a message from Jack Spinner to say that a meeting was being held on Monday and asking whether he had any news, and if not he would call back early Monday afternoon. True to his word, the call came at twenty five minutes past two.

Spinner wasted no time. 'Hello, old boy. There was an MI5 meeting this morning, and our liaison man Monty was in attendance. They've had another report from Manchester, so we are now in possession of names, but still have no idea where exactly they're being housed.'

His response was terse. 'Don't the Met talk to MI5? I can help you with that. Monroe's team traced a text from Samir to Sulamain's mobile. They were in a house in Bermondsey but have done a runner, although they don't know where to at this stage. I'm waiting to get more from him about Sulamain's role in all this.'

Spinner responded, 'Yes, it does sound a bit haphazard, but actually Sulamain, because of his international links, reported to us in MI6 and Samir has been his eyes and ears up in Manchester since he left University at Birkbeck College. That information has not been released to MI5 as yet, so you seem to know more than any one individual at the moment.'

'Thanks a bunch. From being a Good Samaritan I seem to be piggy in the middle all of a sudden. You do realise that Samir's mobile does not seem to be in circulation? If they found out he was texting Sulamain, that could be why Sulamain was topped, and therefore the odds of Samir being around much longer don't amount to much.'

Spinner was contrite. 'Yes, you're right. I'll get Monroe involved in the next meeting. All agencies need to be involved pronto now with one lead co-ordinator. I can assure you, though, that no one knows anything about you at this stage other than that you are an old contact of mine.'

'I would like to keep it that way, if you don't mind,'

'Sure, you can trust me on that one. As a small favour, though, is there any chance you can pop down to London for a few days? What with your knowledge of Manchester and the people up there, I can fill you in on other stuff Sulamain was involved in.'

'What do I tell the girl, not to mention Bill Lambert, which is how all this started?'

'Keep it on a need-to-know basis for now,

and let me know when you check into the Imperial Hotel.'

He began to ask how he knew it was the Imperial, but the line was gone. Jack was a spook, after all.

So Samir had been an agent all along, reporting to his uncle Sulamain. He doubted Jenny or his family knew, but Jenny was bound to be relieved even if her feelings for him had changed. Back to the conservatory, peppermints, and pondering and pacing. He would have to have a talk to Jenny, and maybe try to find out if anything strange had gone on to do with Birkbeck College. Maybe Samir's parents knew something, but how would he explain his asking? He'd never met them, and they probably did not know he existed. Was it a job for Jenny? He would need to meet her before leaving for London, and it would certainly mess up his romantic plans for later in the week.

He decided to telephone Jenny and see if she could meet him that evening for an early dinner. They chose a pizza restaurant in Wilmslow where service was swift and efficient, if not Egon Ronay gold standard. She was enthusiastic about her first day in a new position heading up the conveyancing team, and positively sparkled relating her meeting the latest footballer transferring to

Manchester City FC. He was buying a house in Alderley Edge, and had requested he meet with her at the Etihad Stadium the following Friday, where she would be given a tour. She was not over the moon when the Gent explained that he had to return to London the morning after, but she did agree to be a go-between with Samir's parents. It was not immediately agreed as to how she would be able to explain that whilst his whereabouts were unknown there was no reason to believe at this moment that he was not alive and well. Jenny would also rack her brains to see if there was anything at all that Samir might have said that would help in understanding more about Sulamain or anybody else, old University friends for example, who Samir may have contacted in London.

Jenny was miffed about the date, but had enough on her mind with the new job to be upset for too long. The following day after a meeting in the office she checked her mobile. There was a message from Brightdays Nursing and Care Home to say they had a problem with her granny, and could she call them. Jenny's parents were on holiday in California for three weeks, and Jenny was looking after things in their absence.

Problems come in threes, she thought as she returned the call.

A high sing-song voice answered... 'Good afternoon, Brightdays Nursing and Care Home, how may I help you?'

'I have a message to call Nurse Romero.'

She was transferred promptly. 'Nurse Romero, how can I help you?'

'This is Jenny Lomas. You left me a message.'

'Oh yes, thank you for calling, Jenny. Your grandmother is fine.'

Jenny knew there was a 'but' coming, and the voice became ponderous. She was unable to detect whether this was because the nurse Romero was not conversing in his native language or whether it was an attempt to present the situation in the best light.

'Your grandmother is alright now, but she was found walking through the town centre this morning in her nightgown singing *We'll Meet Again,* and the police have brought her back. She ate all her dinner and the doctor gave her some medication. She's sleeping now. I just wanted to let you know.'

Jenny was lost for words. 'But... but..., how did she get out? There's a passcode for the door.'

'It seems there was a new cleaner and she slipped out while they were transferring equipment to the van,' Romero advised. 'We have new system now. There is a password on internal door as well.'

Jenny could feel a migraine forming. 'OK, I'll be round later.'

When Jenny called round after work, Granny was as bright as a button and could remember nothing of her day out in town, but asked Jenny where her husband John (Jenny's grandfather) was. He had died twenty years before.

On Monday morning, 25ᵗʰ June, on platform one at Crewe railway station, the Gent was duly attired in a Ted Baker suit with a raincoat over his arm, pondering his *Times*. For June it was unusually dark, with a steady drizzle being blown along the platform by the wind-tunnel effect of the platform design. Donning the raincoat, he moved back to stand outside the franchised coffee bar to get more cover. He was reminded of Simon and Garfunkle, and began to whistle to himself the classic song *Homeward Bound*, allegedly written by Paul Simon on that very station – well, one very like it.

His journey on this dismal morning was cheered by an unusual (for him) full English breakfast, which must have been food for the brain, for he used his laptop for more research into Islamic fundamentalism and found that the subject seemed to grow the more one looked into it. From North Africa, where the Tuareg Islamists were muscling in on Mali, to former Soviet satellite states with Muslim populations where developing oil reserves drew more Muslim workers bringing the fundamentalists along with them, the list seemed endless. But the spectre of Al Qaeda was never far away.

He checked in at the Imperial feeling that his knowledge was greatly enhanced, but his understanding no more so. The usual best-buddy rigmarole ensued with the assistant manager, and as he sorted his room out he wondered who he should call first, Monroe or Spinner.

Chapter 21

Samir was still playing his undercover part, but for how much longer? He was sure they must suspect him by now. They must have checked out his mobile, although fortunately he had deliberately not kept his sent messages and he always deleted received messages, so what would they find that was incriminating? Work numbers, girlfriends, family members, and his uncle Sulamain's number? Nothing was incriminating in its own right, although no received messages was obviously suspicious, wasn't it? The routine had now become mind-numbingly boring: prayers were performed as expected, the food was just about OK but when left to the minders it was probably not *halal*. Two of the other 'guests' were plain barking mad, absolute caricatures of terrorists with long black beards, their only topic of conversation being the Koran and *jihad*. Two others, Ahmed and Jumail, from Birmingham, appeared on the surface to be normal and were actually quite intelligent. They were being tutored to get jobs with G4S, the leading international security company, contracted to provide security for the Olympic Games starting on 27th July. G4S had already had significant bad press for not recruiting enough security guards. LOCOG (London Organising Committee of the Olympic and Paralympic Games) would have to rely on the police and the Army to make up the deficit. God knew what mayhem could be in store, should be it left to Ahmed and Jumail.

Meanwhile Ali and Abdullah were truly indoctrinated, being further wound up by Ahmed, Jumail and the barking duo. During any debate, Samir found he was only able to agree, in order not to create suspicion as to his true motives.

It was time for the main meal of the day – nothing extravagant, some white fish and salad. Fish was primarily considered *halal* because of the sayings and actions of the Prophet. Samir had finished his meal when Tariq, one of the minders with a particularly nasty streak, rose from the table, squeezed his shoulder and murmured in his ear.

'I get you some more, my friend.'

Samir shivered. This was not the first time this had happened, and the intention behind the generosity was obvious. He could not recall being over-friendly, but had noticed other guests in the house beginning to converse in easier tones with the minders. Stockholm syndrome, or capture–bonding, was not a figment of imagination; it was happening right there in front of him. He glanced at Ali and Abdullah. It had not gone unnoticed, and he would have to be on his guard.

He recalled the last night in the first house. Late evening, at about ten forty, there had been a loud banging on the door. Before it could be answered a single gunshot was heard and a primeval scream rang out, echoing down the narrow street that was in darkness after a long summer's day. As the door was opened, a minder collapsed through the doorway with blood oozing from a wound in his back. His last words were, 'Help me, help me. They found out.'

Whoever 'they' were and what had been found out was never revealed. All occupants were rounded up and the house was left empty within fifteen minutes.

A van had appeared and they were bundled into the back and had to sit on the floor. The smell suggested it had been used for vegetable deliveries, and in one corner were the remains of a light wooden box, the type used for tomatoes. It was difficult to know where they were being taken, because not much could be seen through the filthy rear windows of the van. They spent the night in the van in some kind of yard. It could not have had anything of value in it, for there were no gates. There was an old caravan and a site hut with running water and a toilet, so perhaps it had been a used car lot at one time. First thing in the morning a man known to Hussein turned up with bread. Later Hussein made a few calls and it transpired another safe house had been found.

In the middle of the morning they were on the Tube heading north of the river. They were to alight at Whitechapel Station for the purpose of buying groceries from Sainsbury's.

The station was opposite the Royal London Hospital on Whitechapel Road. The trio, as UK-born Asians, had never before been to that area of the Capital, and were amazed at the first sights to behold them as they emerged from the underground. For a quarter of a mile to traffic lights on both left and right were Asian shops selling goods of every description, interspersed with restaurants and takeaways and other Asian commercial establishments. At the edge of the wide pavement, their backs to the road, there were also stalls in full competition. This formed a crowded pedestrian thoroughfare with the population mainly Bangladeshi. Many females were in full *burka*, a remarkable sight to behold. Turning left and towards the Mile End Road and Newham, their journey's end, they walked past the Blind Beggar pub, and then left again to Sainsbury's.

From the supermarket they trekked up Mile End Road towards Newham and eventually found the new safe house. It was apparent that the house was already full, with the lounge also functioning as sleeping quarters – not a good omen. Mooching around, they found that an old back kitchen and utility area was vacant. This was commandeered by what was becoming known as Hussein's gang.

The addition of the newcomers made the house overcrowded. Tempers flared owing to the lack of space, and a fight broke out between one of the barking duos and an earlier arrival. This was quickly subdued by a whack on the head with a broom handle from one of the minders, rendering the barking one senseless. Murmurings of dissent with the minders continued until Hussein emerged from the kitchen, black eyes blazing and brandishing a frying pan. Peace was restored; no one messed with Hussein. Samir had noted that he had not been around all the time, but once again his total command had prevented a tense situation turning fatal. The unity was *jihad* alone, even though there were myriad other allegiances.

It wasn't clear whether the others lived here or could return from whence they came. With plenty of time to think, Samir dwelt on their predicament. He wasn't sure if Ali and Abdullah realised their plight, but he concluded that the Manchester group must now be on Britain's most wanted list and would have to be used and discarded – or just plain discarded, one way or another. He shivered at the thought.

The next morning an opportunity occurred. The group were shopping with a minder, as the new house had already run out of food. Ravenous, they ate breakfast in the supermarket café. While waiting to be served, Samir excused himself to use the toilet. There was a phone in the corridor, and he called Sulamain. No answer; he left a message.

'Need to speak urgently, was in Bermondsey, now Whitechapel, calling from Sainsbury's.' Samir scurried back.

The minder quizzed him, 'Are you alright?'

'Yeah, sure, just a bit... you know. I'll be fine after some food.'

He'd thought of doing a runner, but he would surely be seen, and then where would he go anyway? He would hardly go to the police. Would he be better on his own or with Ali and Abdullah? They still appeared totally up for it. All were starving. Breakfast was eaten in near silence, hunger abated.

Chapter 22

The Gent was standing sipping a coffee, staring out at the traffic circling Russell Square. In the distance could be seen the British Museum, Senate House and Telecom Tower. He was also thinking about the Shard when his mobile rang. It was Spinner.

'Good morning, old boy. Are you in London yet?'

'Yes, I'm at the Imperial,' he replied, emerging from a trance.

'Excellent. I'll pop round in an hour, fill you in about Sulamain.'

'OK, see you then. I'll be in the lobby.'

After exchanging pleasantries over tea and biscuits, Spinner began. 'Sulamain came over here from Pakistan with his brother, but rather than join Mansoor in the business he decided to go to university in London. He was bright, and got a first in economics. I initially got to know him in the Politics Society, where he was a fierce debater. When he left, he became a policeman and eventually joined the Met, while I went into the Foreign Office and

187

ended up in MI6. We'd kept in touch from time to time, and when I needed someone with an Asian background, he was perfect. When he retired from the Met and got the job at Harrods that was also very useful. You wouldn't believe how many foreign villains arrive incognito and then blow it all because they like to shop at Harrods. When we wanted to trace someone, it was easy to request a name-check through their customer database and therefore prove where a person was at a particular time. Caught the odd one out, I'll tell you, and saved the bacon of a few more.

'Samir got involved when he was at Birkbeck College, and was disturbed by what a few of his contemporaries appeared to be getting involved in. It was done on an informal basis, relaying odd behaviour or apparent planning of illegal activity, especially of a potentially terrorist nature. This, of course, continued when he went back up to Manchester, although this latest scenario was a bit deeper and now we seem to be in deep shit. We currently have no idea who could have murdered Sulamain, or whether it was connected with the Manchester lot or something else.'

The Gent thought for a moment before responding, 'That's very useful, but not too hot on actual detail Jack, have you anything from Monroe?'

'I've not heard from Monroe as yet. Sulamain's general information passed to us was confirming rises in movements associated with the 'Shia Crescent' – that's a group of Middle East countries where Shia Muslims form a dominant majority. They include Iran, Bahrain and Iraq, and the shape of these countries put together resembles a crescent or half-moon. The large minority Shia hold power in Syria. The phrase 'Shia Crescent' was coined by King Abdullah of Jordan after the fall of Saddam Hussein and the coming to power of a Shiite government in Iraq. Currently the Russians support the Shias. Regarding the civil war in Syria, the militant group there, Hezbollah, and Iran support President Assad's government, whereas the Sunni states of Saudi Arabia, Qatar, and Turkey provide funding and support for the rebels. All this demonstrates that there is great tension between Sunni and Shias spilling over into many other states in the Middle East, and one of the biggest fears is that once the US leaves Iraq, Iran will exert even more influence.'

The Gent was struggling to keep up. 'It was an exceedingly complex subject. And Sulamain was in on this intelligence, although not actually involved. Isn't this what your guys in embassies do? Doesn't seem like enough to get him a knife in the back for his efforts, unless of course you've got a leak and he was fingered.'

Spinner held his hands up. 'A lot of what we do is like that. It's what you do with the information that matters before you send in the action men, but obviously if an agent is compromised then they are in immediate danger. It is always useful to have these opinions confirmed from other sources, especially travellers from those countries. It is certainly not beyond the bounds for Sunnis and Shias to be fighting each other over here.' There was silence for a moment before Spinner continued, 'Where do you think we go from here?'

'It's really your call. Monroe told me about Samir being held in Bermondsey. They traced a text from Samir received on Sulamain's mobile but he didn't say any more as he had another lead but promised to get back to me as soon as.'

Spinner brought the meeting to a close. 'I don't think there's much more we can do for the moment. It might be smoother if we let Monroe come back to you as promised. If you don't hear by the end of the day about this other lead or whatever, let me know. I don't really want to pull rank on him, but tough if we have to.'

Shaking hands, Spinner left and the Gent was left to wait and watch the traffic circling around Russell Square. He had taken on board the Sunni- versus-Shia, thing but it did seem a bit far-fetched for them to be fighting each other in Britain. He decided to go for a walk round Russell Square to mull it all over. As he was walking back into the hotel, Monroe called and said he was on his way. Perhaps the coffee was better in the Imperial.

Half an hour later, Monroe arrived, with Patterson in tow. Settling themselves down, they sipped latte and took a bite of Scottish shortbread. The Gent prayed this wasn't going to be another lecture.

Monroe began. 'I've got something for you: we found evidence that Sulamain was not always the good old boy we thought him to be. Going through his notes and mobile phone records, it appears he was passing on names and details of customers who would be likely to want to go on a *Hajj* to Mecca or wherever. The recipients are an unsavoury gang known to overcharge unsuspecting clients for the privilege of using an Asian tourist agency. The type of client we are talking about here would obviously have money. He got commission of course. The mobile records also show that Samir phoned him from Sainsbury's, in Whitechapel.'

The Gent opened his mouth to speak, but Monroe held his hand up.

'Whoa. We know the rough area but not precise enough, so we can hardly go charging round the streets like storm troopers – that would give the game away and they would be off in minutes.'

The Gent commented, 'That's positive at least. What can you do, though?'

Monroe replied, 'We've got men posted in Sainsbury's and others on the surrounding streets. The problem is we don't know whether they walked or went by car, so it is a bit of a long shot.

'Now, it doesn't help us with who did for Sulamain, as he could just have fallen out with the mob running the *Hajj* scam, but we also found this on his desk, and I'm not sure it was there when we first searched the office.'

He placed a book on the table, entitled *Shia Crescent, Emerging World War III*, by Jamai Haquani. 'Apparently this guy Haquani studied at the University of Kent, he was born and now lives in Alberquerque, New Mexico, and is currently running for the state senate of New Mexico. On Facebook he describes himself as a 'talk-show host, author and analyst with LNG (Local, National and Global)'. Says he studied at University of Kent, Canterbury, United Kingdom, and Hale, Cheshire, United Kingdom... don't know if that means anything. It seems he's an expert on the Middle East, though, and has written lots of books about Islam, Sunnis fighting Shias, etc.'

'That is certainly interesting.' The Gent picked up the book and began to flick over a few pages while Monroe got up to find the bathroom.

Patterson said, 'Got some more information for you, by the way.'

Surprised, he put the book down again to read later. 'Oh? What's that?'

'Remember the black man you asked me about with the missing granddaughter?'

'Yes, of course. Oh no, you don't mean...'

'No, no, nothing like that; at all. You know I told you she came over here to stay with relatives? Well, when she first arrived she was bullied a lot at school, so her uncle, who boxed a bit, took her down to the gym. She didn't really like the boxing – you know fifteen and pretty – but she really took to martial arts; that stuff with throwing metal stars about and banging your fists against the wall. Kung Fu, that's it. Did very well, apparently, and it certainly stopped the bullying anyhow.'

The Gent was confused. 'Where did she

go, then?'

'Hold on, I'm coming to that,' Patterson explained. 'She had a boyfriend who was a bit dodgy, and the family didn't approve. One night after a row she upped and went off with him, just disappeared as I told you before. Heartbroken, they were. Didn't know what had happened to her – well, you saw the grandfather in the station.'

'Yes, I thought he was raving mad.'

Patterson continued, 'True to form, things were fine for a week or so, then she overhead him trying to arrange a party night with a few mates to come around – and she was to be the entertainment. She went ballistic at him and tried to storm out. He grabbed her, she managed to throw a few blows but he was bigger of course and knocked her to the floor. Tough girl: she really lost it at this point. She bit off his nose; she did, and also knocked him unconscious. He's still in hospital.'

'Wow, I hope you're not going to charge her?'

Patterson was smiling now. 'Funny that. The mother of the pimp came in to the station but our desk Sergeant; he's a bit Mutt 'n' Jeff' (deaf) 'and his record-keeping… well.'

'So how has it all ended up?'

'All is peace and light now. She came back tail between her legs, but all settled now. She's back at school, doing her exams, wants to go to university and be a doctor.'

A minute later the chief inspector returned, finished his shortbread, and as there was nothing further to say at this point they bade farewell, promising to keep in touch when he found out more about where Samir was being held.

After they'd gone, the Gent picked up the Jamai Haquani book about the 'Shia Crescent' and began flicking through pages again, but found no great inspiration. His mind kept wandering to the Shard. He had a few hours to spare; he'd been sat in the hotel room long enough. Picking up his mobile and a telescopic umbrella, he set off briskly for Russell Square Tube station. Clouds were circling. He took the Piccadilly line one stop to Holborn, changed to the Central line to Bank, and finally travelled south on the Northern to London Bridge. It wasn't a long trek, but preoccupied as he was he had no recollection of the actual journey.

The brolly was folly. – *Funny – not,* he thought, as it was bright sunshine outside the Tube station in the London Bridge Quarter. The internet blurb and websites for the 'Shard' and the 'Place', another new construction, together with London Bridge station itself, described a futuristic utopian environment, but in the summer of the year 2012 this was yet to be fulfilled. Strolling up Borough High Street and turning left into St Thomas's Street, he was able to see a good distance down towards Bermondsey Street, and it seemed that with the left side of the street plastered with construction hoardings and the Shard still under construction, there was still some way to go to reach that utopian goal. A short distance down St Thomas's Street, he branched left up an escalator and onto a piazza outside the Shard, giving entry into the station and with a view of the Place on the other side of Joiner Street. Wandering around the piazza, it was still difficult to feel an affinity with the use of the descriptive 'quarter' when used for buildings rather than culture or ethnicity. He peered into the various station entrances and looked up and down Joiner Street and London Bridge Street, then turning a full circle he stared at the Place and marvelled at the height of the Shard. Adjusting his vision to the brightness, he strolled bravely over to the entrance of the Shard, where a very tall dark-suited black man with shades stood at sentry. Feigning a Northern accent, he asked, 'Ahem, excuse me for being thick, but I know this is the Shard building, but what exactly is the London Quarter?'

In an unexpectedly cultured accent, the black man replied, 'It's all of this lot, sir.'

'Including the building over the road?'

'Yes Sir.'

'And what is in the Shard?'

'Everything you want, sir: offices, shops, apartments, a hotel, restaurants.'

'Can you just come in and take a look?'

'I'm afraid not, sir, certainly not at the moment. You would need to book or make an appointment.'

'Right OK. Thanks very much.'

With that he went on his way back to London Bridge Tube station. The journey to Russell Square was spent thinking about the London Bridge Quarter and the Shard in particular, but he arrived back at the Imperial still confused and uninspired.

Chapter 23

On the way back to the house, Samir took careful note of where they were going. He missed the actual street name, but it was off the Mile End Road towards Newham. If he could get to a phone he could describe their whereabouts in much more detail. The overcrowding problem was solved that day when all transferring occupants from the first house, save for the trio, were shipped out. To where was not explained. This did reduce the tension and propensity for rebellion, but the trio still had no idea of what their mission was to be. All requests for information on the subject were met with a bland reply of 'you will be advised soon', which wasn't very helpful.

They ate reasonably well that night after the shopping trip, with fresh chicken in a curry made by one of the minders who had once worked in a restaurant. It was complemented with salad and poppadums' with all the trimmings. The original occupants even began to converse with 'them from up North', as they were termed.

There was still no mention of names in the

press, and they wondered how long this would continue. It was indeed strange that the Sword of Allah incident had hardly been discussed between them, as though by not being mentioned it had not actually happened. They were all homesick by now, and missing their families. Ali was the more reflective and emotional, and first talked about his mother and aunt and how they could not speak English, before voicing his opinion on the continued subjugation of females in their culture: lack of education, marriage opportunities, etc., which ensured that they remained trapped like moles communicating via tunnels from one section of their community to the other, with little interaction to the world outside.

Ali and Abdullah continued to speculate on the mission and discuss bomb strategy and kidnap techniques. They were still revolutionaries and *jihadists*. The word 'terrorist' was never used among them, and they strangely skirted around the potential of dead bodies as though this could not be a result of their actions.

The next day, Hussein came back to the house, having visited the mosque, and advised that Ibrahim Abelgadar was preaching on Friday and would want to meet with them afterwards. This exciting news pervaded the atmosphere and lifted spirits for the rest of the week.

Unfortunately, history was about to repeat itself. Inevitably in a closeted, all-male situation, the lack of female company had been raised. Unbeknown to the trio and Hussein, one the minders, who was part of a trafficking gang, had arranged for a couple of their girls to be brought round for the night. They were white, obviously underage and vulnerable – probably runaways from care homes, and well drugged up. Both were giggling and appeared tipsy as well, one carrying an alcopop drink. They were spirited into a back room.

There was a mixed reaction. Some of the men were interested and were only too eager to participate in what was the organised rape of underage girls, while the more zealous occupants were angry and astounded that there were such thugs and low-life in their midst. Tension was mounting, and the most pious were baying for blood. No one had seen Hussein – he was out the back and must have heard the commotion. He came storming into the main room, and the trio were automatically drawn to his side. It only took seconds to assess the situation, and the battle lines had already been drawn.

Hussein screamed, 'Out, you infidels and whoremongers, defilers of children, into the street!'

The two thugs posing as minders stood their ground. The trio had no weapons, although Samir could rely on his martial arts, Abdullah was a bear, and Ali grabbed a folding chair. Curses were made, fingers pointed, and grappling ensued and spilled out into the street. One minder drew a knife and that was it: Hussein roared, an erupting volcano, and the Sword of Allah was drawn again. It was no metaphor: there was blood on the street, and neighbours called the police. It was over in minutes, and the girls were placed in the care of two of the more pious ones until the police arrived. Fortunately, no one was killed but the casualty department at the local hospital would be busy that night.

They regrouped and there were groans all round as Hussein advised them that they were on the move again. Blood was seeping through his shirt from a gash on his sword arm, Samir was limping from a kick to the thigh, and Ali had a cut to the head where his own weapon, the metal chair, had been wrestled from his grasp and used against him.

The next house was not far away. Samir in particular wondered who owned all these houses and why there were so many single young men needing short-term accommodation. The wondering didn't last long: concerns about how he could extricate himself from the mess he was in quickly came flooding back. He had to get back to his uncle somehow.

Chapter 24

It was Wednesday, and Jenny was at her lady improver's class at Forest View Golf Club. There were only six that morning, and the pro Billy Wills was able to give each plenty of time. Her play around the green had come on in leaps and bounds since purchasing the lob wedge. The major problem now was a slice to the right, the scourge of many golfers, caused mostly by an out to in-swing. Billy was in full flow, enjoying the limelight surrounded by six adoring females hanging on his every word.

'Reduce the back swing, keep the right arm in, make sure you follow through and don't move your head,' he prattled.

Jenny wasn't sure if was a lecture or a sermon, but even when she remembered, it never seemed to work. Her drives off the tee were all a bit of a lottery, and the video she had been given basically confirmed it was practice, practice and more practice that was required. The golf joke ascribed to an old pro as to why he was so good came to mind: *I'm just lucky, I guess, but the more I practise the luckier I get.*

Coffee and biscuits were included in the cost of the lesson, and she chatted aimlessly with two other girls, Heidi and Sarah, dressed in matching golf gear from Golfino of Wilmslow. They always had plenty of time for golf and didn't seem to work. Perhaps they were WAGs.

Heidi was nosey, 'Jenny, what's happened to that nice fella who used to coach you a bit? I've not seen him around for a while. I thought you and he seemed to be getting on, a bit old-fashioned but such a gentleman.'

'Oh, he's had a lot of business to attend these last few weeks, but I'm sure he'll be back soon, and you know I'll keep you up to date.'

Heidi got the message and the conversation turned to Harvey Nichols's Manchester half-price sale.

Jenny had taken the day off work, and in the afternoon she was due to see Samir's parents again. Driving back to Wilmslow, she was apprehensive about her reception. As far as she knew, there had been no news about Samir, which was now appearing strange after all the time that had elapsed. The murder of Sulamain, Mansoor's brother, would have further added to their tragedy.

After showering, she changed out of her

golf outfit, opting for jeans and a jumper. Not feeling hungry after the coffee and biscuits at the golf club, she skipped lunch and munched on a banana whilst driving over to the Khan house in Wilmslow.

Aisha opened the door and ushered her inside. Although smartly dressed in a traditional sari, she looked tired and wan. Going into the lounge, Mansoor had obviously not worked that morning dressed as he was, wearing a checked shirt, jeans and loafers. Touching cheeks, she could smell whisky. A little early, she determined.

Where to begin? Jenny thought, but fortunately Mansoor was the first to speak.

'Do you have any news for us?' he enquired.

'No, I'm afraid not,' Jenny responded. 'I'm very sorry to hear about your brother Sulamain.'

Aisha began to wail, 'First Samir is missing; now Sulamain has been murdered. What is the world coming to?'

Mansoor tried to reassure his grief-stricken wife, handing her a handkerchief. 'Try and be calm, dear. Jenny is also upset but she is here to help us find Samir.'

Aisha blew her nose and spoke as her eyes welled with tears again. 'Yes, yes, of course I will try. Please ask us anything, anything at all that will help to find Samir.'

Jenny tentatively said, 'I have been thinking, is it possible he could have contacted friends from his university days at Birkbeck College? Can you remember anybody in particular that he would still be friends with, and would you have their contact details anywhere?'

Mansoor answered, 'I'm not sure. His old laptop computer is still upstairs, so I could trawl through that – emails and things – and also check if there are any notebooks. He did have a Filofax as well in those days.'

'That would be excellent,' Jenny said. 'Do you think you could let me know later?'

'Yes, of course,' Mansoor agreed.

Driving back home, Jenny felt true sorrow for Aisha and Mansoor, but strangely only a distant fondness for Samir, as though a door had closed, never to be reopened. She vowed to herself that she would still do all she could to find him.

Jenny was having a busy day, but before going home she called in to see her granny at Brightdays Nursing and Care Home. Granny was normally in the lounge watching TV in the late afternoon, but apparently she had fallen a few days before and was still in bed recovering. She had also been refusing food and had lost weight. The nurse assured her that things were fine and she would improve. Conversation was minimal, with the same topic being repeated several times over. Jenny tried to be upbeat, but drove away in tears and feeling totally drained. *Why does this happen? It's not right*, she thought. She was beginning to understand what her parents were going through. Her granny was not the person she remembered from childhood, and there was the financial burden too: the room cost £800 per week, and the National Health Service had ruled that Granny did not meet the criteria for funding. 'You bastards' she cursed, slamming her fist onto the steering wheel. 'Jobsworths, with tick boxes,' she continued, causing the young couple in the Ford Fiesta next to her in the outside lane at the traffic lights to turn and stare before exchanging smirks as they waited for the lights to change. Her anger only increased as she considered the unfairness of having to sell Granny's house in order to pay for the care-home bills. It was no wonder 'grey power' was mobilising.

Back home she poured a decent glass of wine and put a Marks & Spencer ready meal for one in the oven. The blurb sounded good: 'Farm-reared, free-range, corn-fed chicken with shallots in red wine, accompanied by Lyonnais potatoes and asparagus'. She could almost hear the sweet, purring voice of the woman doing the voice-over from the telly ad. There was an inane American sitcom on the TV, but watching the planes take off from nearby Manchester airport was more interesting. She poured another glass of wine, and the oven timer pinged; the meal wasn't bad and the sitcom seemed better – or was it just the wine?

The evening was in full swing now. *Coronation Street* was on: Ken Barlow's mutt had fallen in the canal. Riveting stuff! Thankfully at that moment the phone rang, so she put the TV on mute. It was Mansoor, who'd found some useful information on the laptop.

'There are some names in the old Filofax that I seem to remember Samir talking about – going to watch cricket at the Oval, that sort of thing. No addresses but at least phone numbers and landlines as well. Have you got a pen ready? Will Johnson and Brian Foster.'

She hurriedly wrote down the names and numbers. 'That's fantastic. I'll get onto it immediately and let you know what I can find out.'

She thought for a moment and called the Gent with the news.

He picked up straightaway.

'You have done well! But let's not build our hopes up just yet. I'll give them a call tonight and see what's what. I also have news about Sulamain. He related the details given by Spinner and Monroe, leaving out the bit about Sulamain's dealings in the dodgy travel-agency business.'

'So we still have no idea as to anyone he could have crossed?'

Ah! He thought. I *could be caught out here. No point trying to shield her from the truth.* He told her about the *Hajj* scam, but asked her not to reveal it to Mansoor just yet.

'No of course not, I understand. You'll let me know if you find anything.'

'Yes, as soon as I've got something,' he said, and rang off.

The Gent thought for a moment and decided there was no time like the present. He could at least call them with the honest explanation that Samir was not in touch with his parents and that they had asked him to help in finding his whereabouts.

He called Will Johnson first. A woman answered, who turned out to be his mother. Will had moved out some weeks before and now lived in Brighton, but she was able to provide a mobile number. Writing it down, he reassured her that there was nothing untoward before thanking her and ringing off. Brighton was a bit of a trek, but it had to be worth a call. He rang the mobile number, but left a message when it wasn't answered.

Brian Foster next: it rang for a long time. He was expecting an answerphone message to kick in, but then a young male voice answered, 'Look, Cheryl, I've apologised a thousand times. Why don't I come round?'

'I'm not Cheryl,' he said with amusement.

'No, sorry,' the young male said. 'I've been having a bit of a spat with the girlfriend for the last hour or so. Who are you after?'

'Brian Foster,' he replied.

'Don't know him, but then I only moved in two weeks ago. There's three other blokes live here. They're not in yet – probably still in the pub. I'll get someone to call you back, shall I?'

'Yes, thank you, that would be great,' he said, leaving his own number.

He received a call an hour later. He picked up, wondering whether it would refer to Will or Brian, as he was not expecting anyone else. Luck: it was to do with Brian.

'Looking for Brian Foster,' a man announced, in a strong Scots brogue.

'Yes. Can you help me?'

'Depends who you are I guess, and why you looking for him.'

Detecting some reluctance, he explained the situation.

'Oh. Never met this Samir fella, but I remember they were mates at Birkbeck. I can give you a mobile number – not been much use to me, though. Brian moved out a month ago, owing me money for his electricity and gas. Maybe you'll have better luck.'

As he wrote the number down and thanked the Scot, he wondered whether he might have more success given that finance was not involved.

It was now eight o'clock, so probably worth a try.

It was answered immediately. 'Brian Foster,' the voice announced in a clear North London accent.

He explained as briefly as possible the situation of looking for Samir on behalf of his parents.

Brian was as helpful as could be expected, confirming that in their university years they had lived in the same halls of residence but contact since had been sporadic, adding, 'He did phone me a couple of months ago wanting to get together for a catch up, but I've moved since then and changed my mobile number so he may be a bit behind. He didn't seem himself, somehow though: he sounded far too serious. Not getting married, is he? Anyway, that's all I know. Tell him to contact me if you find him.'

'I'm sure he'll be pleased to get back in touch.' Proffering thanks, the Gent ended the conversation.

He considered the conversation with Brian Foster. Could any more be expected from Will Johnson, assuming he even responded? His thoughts went back to Samir.

If Samir could not contact his uncle's office, he would not be able to contact his parents either, so surely he would try his uncle's house first? Was there an aunt and children? What had Harrods had to say about the murder? Mohamed al-Fayed, the owner of Harrods and a larger-than-life character, was no shrinking violet. Monroe was being a bit slow here, after originally promising to be a good buddy. He must have more information by now. It was ten o'clock. He decided to sleep on it and he would ring Monroe first thing in the morning.

It could have been a coincidence, but Samir's thoughts were in parallel. Should he do a runner, which would, a) jeopardise the mission, b) blow his cover, and c) have repercussions for Ali and Abdullah. The general plods would be unlikely to believe him, certainly not straightaway. Could he hide away somewhere? He'd had a few beers with his old college mate Will Johnson a few weeks back, and the last time he'd tried to contact him his mother said he'd moved out and was living in Brighton, but at that stage she only had a mobile number which, when he tried, did not seem to be working. Will had been providing information for Sulamain via Samir about a dodgy travel agents, a throwback to work they had undertaken for Sulamain whilst at university. Will must be in danger, otherwise he would not have moved. Was he trying to make contact?

What a mess, he thought. It all went back to Sulamain. He must be trying to find the safe house, presumably with the assistance of

Met detectives. He resolved to try and ring again, or perhaps ring Sulamain's house not far from Wimbledon Common, where his Aunt Shakira spent many hours walking her pedigree Afghan hound. He would have to be cautious, though, for she was totally unaware of his role in reporting intelligence to Sulamain.

Chapter 25

The Gent woke early and breakfasted in his room, flicking through the *Times*. There had been no further mention of the Manchester takeaway incident, and neither was there speculation as to whether the Greater Manchester police knew the names of any suspects, and if so why they had not been released to the press.

Regarding international news, all the papers were full of the Syrian army murdering their own people, whether rebels, insurgents or they just happened to be in the way at the time. It was a civil war, and refugee camps were appearing in Lebanon and Turkey. It could be Sunni against Shia. There was also a piece about people abseiling down the Shard building. Rumour had it that Prince Andrew might be having a go.

It was time to call Monroe.

He answered grumpily. 'Monroe. Ah, good morning, I've been meaning to get back to you. I've got a bit more news for you, yes. Harrods spokesperson can't shed any light onto why Sulamain was murdered, but did say that he had been open about him giving names to this travel agent as part of his connection with MI6. Seems they kind of approved. Could be more to it, because if they are dodgy with people and stuff going out, they are likely to be dodgy with people and stuff coming in, if you get my drift.'

'Yes,' he replied. 'All sounds logical when it's spelt out like that.'

'The jury's still out as to when the news of Sulamain's death should be released to the media, and of course Samir doesn't know yet either, so we need to have some kind of story next time he makes contact, which he has to do soon. We're pretty close now as to his whereabouts. There was some kind of fight at the house, but they'd scarpered again before we got there, although we don't think they went far because we'd been keeping tabs on an old Toyota van that they abandoned a mile away. His last call was from Sainsbury's, so my guess is that's where he'll try from again. We've got a couple of men undercover there, but we have got be careful not to blow Samir's cover.'

'Yes, I agree. At least we seem to be closing in now, and once we have eyeball I assume you can control the situation.'

Monroe was more circumspect. 'Well, we could if we knew what exactly they were planning to do. If what was planned was wholesale murder, we obviously could not allow that, but we do need to catch them in the act, so to speak, in order for all charges to stick.'

The Gent interjected, 'I've got a few questions. You've not said anything about Sulamain's mobile, which is presumably what Samir is likely to try calling on again. Is it still working? If not, he'll be suspicious, and if he calls Sulamain's home he'll expect Sulamain to be there. Do you want Harrods to be talking to Samir or what? It would be better, perhaps, if you routed calls from the mobile to a dedicated policemen or agent who Samir would be likely to trust. Do you know whether Samir knew about Jack Spinner, or Harry Farquarson as he was known?

Monroe replied testily, 'I have been working on all that. I've been trying to get a meeting with Jack Spinner, but not having much success right now. Would you like to be included?'

'Why, yes, of course. Thank you,'

'OK, I'll come back to you,' Monroe said as he rang off.

The Gent reflected. He didn't want to upset Monroe, but Samir was becoming central to any chance of a positive outcome to the dilemma. Spinner might know more, and

GMP might know more by now. His next call would be to Lambert. He hadn't worked so hard for a long time, and it felt good.

Before calling Lambert he collected his thoughts, picked up his laptop and went up to the Imperial's Atrium coffee bar for elevenses and internet Wi-Fi facilities. After checking emails, something was still niggling, at the back of his mind: of course, why had no one mentioned Sulamain's wife, Samir's aunt? By 'someone', he meant Monroe. It stood out a mile that she would have been one of the first people to have been informed, and she would also have had to identify the body. Monroe was either incompetent or keeping something back. The promised meeting with him and Spinner was going to be interesting...

Frank Smith was the leader of KNI (Knights of New Islington). He was leader because he probably had three marbles as opposed to the others' three between them. He got his nickname 'Fwankie' from being constantly referred to as such by Lenny, a black lad who stood at a shade less than six feet, not especially tall in this day and age. What made Lenny distinctive, however, was his remarkable likeness to 'Iron' Mike Tyson, ex-world champion heavyweight boxer. He was not pretty, and very tough, but definitely not the sharpest knife in the box. The gang needed an enforcer, and most people crossed the street when Lenny came along.

The gang members of KNI and most of the other young men they associated with had never worked. In fact, they came under the government classification of NEET (Not in Employment, Education or Training). Many of them came from households where nobody had ever worked: a sad reflection on the previous Labour government's social engineering policies – equality and diversity, health and safety, and the like. One of the saddest was the channelling of funds into deprived areas, which resulted in successful training centres having to close, with redundancies, simply because new contracting rules meant that funding was withdrawn if the centre was not located within the boundaries of a deprived area. This and other similar benefits had the opposite effect of that desired, by reinforcing a ghetto culture in which young people were discouraged from looking outwards and seeking work and other opportunities outside of their immediate environment.

KNI were having a night out that evening. They could stay overnight in a large council flat so long as they kept reasonably quiet. Lenny's elder brother had recently got himself shacked up with a girl, who had, courtesy of the council, a nice three-bed pad for her and her two-year-old. It was a meeting of the Knights – shame it wasn't a round table, but at least they called the pub the Round House. The place was in Wythenshawe, the sprawling ghetto area on the south side of Manchester famed for sink estates. Close to Manchester International Airport, it might be another country, hemmed in as it mostly was by motorways. They had the plan and had agreed to do the job. The bloke who had financed them would have the means. They were to collect the petrol bombs and chuck them through the windows of Manchester City Football Club at the Etihad Stadium. The strange thing was they never bothered to ask why – perhaps the thought never occurred!

Inspector Bill Lambert of GMP was in a good mood. He had just come out of a CTU (Counter Terrorism Unit) meeting, which had gone quite well considering they still had no result with the Sword of Allah incident, but at least the perpetrators were now in London and the responsibility of the Met and MI5. Assistant Chief Constable Henry Partridge had commented favourably to Malcolm Brampton, CTSA from the CTB Ports Unit, about the apprehension of wanted terrorists trying to slip into the country via Manchester Airport. Lambert himself and Shug (Shugofta Rahman, CTSA) got brownie points for the swift arrest of three members of KNI (Knights of New Islington) after petrol bombs had been thrown through several windows at the Etihad Stadium in the early hours of the previous Saturday morning in an attempt to disrupt Manchester City's scheduled match that day. KNI's plan had been to create a large fire, but the area they had chosen was guarded by fire protection sprinklers, which detected the fire before it could take hold. They also hadn't known that the systems were sophisticated, so that only those sprinklers necessary to control the particular area of the fire would go off, thereby also reducing water damage. Shug had done most of the legwork after following up leads during her night-time patrol, and Lambert was particularly proud, as he had been her mentor.

'You're chirpy this morning, Bill,' the Gent declared.

'Yes, had a good meeting earlier. The boss was pleased with a couple of results we got.'

Lambert related the topics of the meeting, and they concluded that there was no bearing on the London investigation.

The Gent's mind was still buzzing. He

pressed the contact buttons on his mobile and Jenny answered.

'Hi, good morning, how are things?'

'Excellent. Had a successful meeting this morning with Sevez Pelotti, the new Man City footballer I was telling you about. He's going ahead with that house in Alderley Edge – £2.5m! I tell you, the drinks are on me when my commission comes in! Roberto Mancini, the manager, wants me to find him something now as well. How is that?'

'Wow, that's fantastic. You must be doing a great job. What does the boss have to say? Mine is champagne, by the way.'

'OK no problem although it might not be actual champagne. The boss is happy so far, but he is a bit of a cold fish. You phoned me, by the way, or did you just want to chat?'

'Well, of course, but I'm thinking: no one down here is saying much about Samir's uncle and nothing at all about his Aunt Shakira. The police have said nothing, and yet they must have been round to see her. She must have identified the body and all that. I was wondering if you could see what you could find out about her from the parents. You seem to have developed a good rapport with them.'

Jenny was honest. 'You know, I never thought to ask about anything other than Samir himself, but it does make sense that he may have said something or tried to contact the family. I'll get in touch with them today, and you're right, I think they will talk to me again. It may be tonight or even tomorrow before I call you back, though, as I have an evening appointment.'

'OK, soon as you can, then. And thanks.'

Jenny actually phoned back that evening.

'The Khans were only too willing to talk to me if it would help in locating Samir. Get this: Shakira is a partner in a travel agency specialising in arranging *Hajj* trips to Mecca, and from what you said about Sulamain and his dubious connections that sounds a bit dodgy, don't you think?'

'It certainly bears some scrutiny, that's for sure. You didn't perhaps happen to get an address or phone number, by any chance, did you?'

'Yes, I did. Have you got your pen ready?'

He gratefully wrote down the details. 'Excellent work, Jenny, I think I had better have a chat with Chief Inspector Monroe in the morning, see if he knows any more. Bye for now.'

Address and phone number was one thing, but he could hardly go ringing up out of the blue days after her husband had been murdered. He would have to presume upon Monroe for the moment. After all, it might have nothing at all to do with the crooked minders, and there were loads of travel agents in London booking trips to Mecca.

Monroe was forthcoming about having informed Shakira Khan about the demise of her husband Sulamain. She had predictably broken down at the news, as had the two sons Amir and Latif, who were both in their twenties. She confirmed that she was a partner in a travel agency called Mideast Travel Limited. Arranging *Hajj* pilgrimages was a multimillion-pound business, with costs ranging from £3,000 to £5,000 for one person. The Saudis kept a quota system on how many pilgrims from the United Kingdom could visit in any one year, and it was currently 25,000. By what was currently known, there was no connection with any dodgy minders keeping a check on Samir and the other inhabitants of the various safe houses. Fraud was quite common, and had featured on the BBC news programme where unwitting pilgrims had parted with money to bogus operators, some of whose business premises turned out to be empty shops. Others found no accommodation had been booked for them when they arrived in Mecca.

Back at the Imperial, the Gent was pondering on what Monroe had said about Shakira Khan and the travel agency business. He would have liked to have a word with her, but on what pretext? Surely she knew Samir was missing, and how big a part did she play in the actual running of the agency? He had the contact details from Jenny. Doubt caused him to pause as he picked up the phone and he called Jenny instead. She was at work, but things were quiet, as it was Friday.

With no time to waste he said, 'Hi, it's me. I'm sorry to rush you, but when you spoke to Mansoor and Aisha about Samir's Aunt Shakira, how did they feel about her? Had they been in touch? Could you tell what kind of relationship they had?'

Jenny answered honestly, 'I didn't have time to tell you everything before. They had spoken briefly and offered condolences, and she had advised that she had not seen or spoken to Samir for months. To be frank, they didn't appear to like her very much, but why I don't know. Do you think that's important?'

He was equally uncertain. 'I don't know either way, but it's definitely worth finding out. Look, I've got an idea: if I make contact, she's likely to tell me to sling my hook, but if you were with me as Samir's girlfriend, with a pledge to Aisha and Mansoor to try and find

Samir, she may just give us the time of day. Is there any chance you can finish early and hightail it down here and I'll make the arrangements as soon as?'

Jenny was all for it. 'Yeah, this all getting exciting, and I did meet her once so I think she would be OK about it. With it being the weekend, there will be no problems with work, and I can stay longer if necessary because I've got lots of holiday to take before my boss leaves and I take up the reins and managing the conveyancing department. I'll get the next train from Manchester Piccadilly to Euston. I'll get on at Stockport, and I'll call Shakira while I'm on the train and explain the situation.'

'Call me when you get to Euston, and I'll get a table booked for dinner. Look forward to seeing you. Take care.'

Jenny managed to get off work early on the pretext of having to visit her granny. First she hurried home and slung her work clothes into the washer. After a quick freshen-up she threw a few things into an overnight bag and set off for Stockport to get the first train to London Euston.

The Gent was unsure whether to confide in Monroe or just wing it. Monroe didn't appear to have got much information from Shakira, other than the obvious fact about being a partner in the travel agency, which she could hardly have denied. He also wondered about the boys' relationship with Samir, and whether they had anything to do with the agency.

At five forty-five, his mobile sounded. He thought it was Jenny arriving at Euston.

'It's me, Amelia. Can you talk?' She sounded tearful.

'Yes, of course. What's happened?'

'He's at it again. He's been in the gallery again, twice last week. He's getting very familiar, trying to get close when I'm not behind my desk, and said I had a nice house. How does he know that?' at which she burst into tears.

He was at a loss: she was in Cheshire, and he was in London, up to his neck. What could he say to pacify her? What could he advise? Before he could speak, she recovered and stammered again.

'And last night I'm sure I saw him in the street outside, staring at the house. I'm frightened he'll try something, and I've just seen him again and I've only just got here. Did he follow me home?'

He felt any response other than agreement would only increase her anxiety. He was reluctant to raise the topic, but nothing had been mentioned about any reaction from her partner Josephine, although he knew that things had been a bit rocky for a couple months now owing to Jo's paranoid jealousy and propensity to violence, as might be expected from a Thai kick-boxer.

'Ahem. What does Jo have to say about this man?' he ventured.

Amelia's reply was blunt. 'She moved out! Anyway, you know what she's like; she would have just gone out and beaten him to a pulp. And what use would that have been? Oh! She took the cat as well, the bitch.'

Enough said, he thought. *It's time to move on.* 'Well, I suppose at least it might have stopped him. I'm sure you are right, though: something needs to be done now! Someone needs to confront him, but not you of course. What did the police have to say?'

Back in control now, Amelia replied, 'Well, they were very sympathetic, but came out with the standard line that until he actually did something their hands were tied. How naff is that?'

'Yes,' he agreed, 'but in my opinion he has now actually done 'something' by standing outside your house.'

'But what do I do now?'

'I'm stuck down here for a few days, but I think you need to do two things: one, speak to your boss and tell him everything you have just told me and insist that he confronts the man in your presence the next time he comes into the gallery, and two, go back to the police and tell them the latest and can they give you a direct number to ring if he appears at the house again. Oh! And can you also ring that number for when he comes in the gallery, as if they are quick enough they might get round before he goes. And if all else fails, you could always go and stay with your sister for a while.'

Amelia was relieved. 'Yes, that sounds like positive action, so long as my boss and the police go along with it.'

He was relieved that she sounded less stressed.

'I'll get onto it right now and thank you so much for guiding me in the right direction.'

'It is always easier from the outside looking in. Let me know how it goes.'

'Yes, I will, and thank you once again. Bye.'

Still concerned, he placed his mobile back on the table.

He was still thinking about the situation fifteen minutes later when Jenny phoned from Euston.

He answered eagerly. 'You're earlier than I expected. That's great.'

Jenny was equally keen. 'Yes, I managed to get on an earlier train that was running late. I should be about half an hour. I spoke to Shakira. She's still in bits, but said to call around in the morning.'

'Well done. I'll get the gin and tonics on ice.'

'She also said that the police didn't seem to be getting very far in finding out who killed Sulamain, and as we had been asked by Samir's parents to try and find him could we also find out who murdered Sulamain.'

'Whoa, slow down a moment,' he said. 'Theorising about terrorist plots and Samir's whereabouts is one thing, but we can hardly traipse about London pretending to be the

Met. Then again, we've done alright so far, not being hidebound by health and safety and such. We can do things our own way without worrying about rules and filling loads of forms in like the Met would have to do... I'll tell you what: let's think about it overnight. Maybe after talking to Shakira tomorrow we'll know more, have a better idea how to play it.'

He was not quite over the shock of Sheila's death yet, but the prospects of a few days of Jenny's company made him fuss about like a teenager, until the realisation became embarrassing and he made an effort to concentrate on the problems at hand. Perhaps tomorrow's meeting would provide some insight.

Still obviously in deep mourning and dressed accordingly, Shakira welcomed them into the detached house in a quiet avenue close to Wimbledon Common. They were fiercely welcomed by two large Afghan hounds, still damp from their walk on a drizzly morning. With dark hair and deep brown eyes that commanded attention, Shakira was definitely not a sleeping partner in the travel agency business. He was introduced as a friend of both Jenny and

Samir. Amir was out but Latif offered to make coffee.

Shakira spoke first. 'Please forgive me if I can't keep this up for long.'

Jenny's sympathy was natural and unforced. 'We totally understand, and if at any time you wish to stop, please just say and we will leave immediately.'

Shakira nodded. 'Thank you, but we don't even know when the inquest will be yet. They still have to do an autopsy or a post-mortem or something yet. That policeman said no burial can be planned for the time being. It's awful.'

She glanced over at Latif to pour coffee.

'Inspector Monroe?' he asked.

'Yes,' confirmed Shakira. 'Look, I know Aisha and Mansoor have asked you to help find Samir, but do you think you could also help to find Sulamain's killers?'

Boxed into a corner, they confirmed simultaneously, 'Yes, of course we will.'

The Gent followed with, 'You do realise that the Met had me in their sights as a suspect when I went to see Sulamain to ask about Samir's whereabouts?'

'Oh, I am sorry. I had no idea. Does that mean you won't help me?'

He was well and truly boxed in now. 'No of course not; it is the least we can do as we are already, shall we say, on the case in view of helping the Met with their enquiries – in the broadest sense of the word, of course.'

Shakira was obviously grateful. 'What would you like to ask me?'

Jenny began hesitantly. 'You know we have been speaking to Samir's parents about trying to find him... has he contacted you at all?'

'No,' Shakira responded. 'I've not spoken to him for some time.'

'I understand you are a partner in a travel agency?'

'Yes, I am,' Shakira answered. 'Latif works for me there, and Amir, my other son, works in a bank.'

The Gent had further questions. 'Did Sulamain have anything to do with the day-to-day running of the agency?'

'No, he was a director and shareholder of the company but did not work on a day-to-day basis.'

He probed further. 'Were you aware that Sulamain provided names and contact details to another agency for a commission?'

Shakira was a little guarded. Latif was about to speak, but she waved her hand to convey she was prepared to answer. 'Yes, of course I was. We specialise in *Hajj* trips for Shia pilgrims wishing to visit shrines in Iraq, mostly the cities of Najaf and Karbala. My understanding is that the other agency would specialise mainly in trips for Sunni Muslims to Mecca and Medina in Saudi Arabia.'

He thought some light was dawning. 'Has Inspector Monroe offered any ideas as to why someone would want to harm your husband, Shakira?'

Shakira was constantly dabbing her eyes now. 'No nothing at all. It's so...' Her voice trailed off, and Latif came to the rescue.

He spoke calmly but conclusively, 'I really think we need to end it there.'

There was nothing more to be said, and with promises to advise of any news, they left Shakira and Latif to their grieving.

Back at the hotel, Jenny queried, 'I know we couldn't say no to Shakira, but how exactly do we go about solving Sulamain's murder?'

'Good question,' he said. 'Right now I don't know. I think we need to find out more about the agency and what role Latif plays in it, and also what information Harrods may have to offer. Will you call Shakira and see if we can have a chat with Latif, preferably at the agency, whilst I try Harrods.'

He wondered why Monroe had not said much about what Harrods had to say about the murder of Sulamain, and decided to call him first.

The chief inspector was in, but in a foul mood. 'Monroe,' he growled.

The Gent, in his politest voice, announced himself, 'Good morning, Chief Inspector. I was wondering if you could just help me with something.'

'What do you want? I'm busy,' he retorted.

'Well, Shakira has asked me if I have any ideas about Sulamain's murder, and I was wondering what Harrods had to say.'

He could hear the steam coming out of Monroe's ears.

'Bloody hell, are you calling the shots now, eh? You shouldn't be anywhere near a police investigation, really, and it's only because of your friends at MI6 that I'm talking to you at all!' Monroe's own words did the trick, and he calmed down a little. 'Well, what did you want to know?'

Pleased, the Gent posed some obvious but potentially incisive questions. 'Firstly, did they think he had any enemies? Was he a good employee? Stuff like that. Were they happy that his wife ran a travel agency and that he provided the agency with names of Harrods customers who could be potential customers of the agency?'

Monroe was upfront. 'The Met's remit is to find the perpetrators, full stop. We're not interested whether he was a good employee, or even if he passes information to his wife's agency, unless of course it impinges on the investigation. So in short, they don't know Jack-whatsit.'

'I'm beholden to you,' he replied. 'Just one more thing: could I drop your name if they are reluctant to talk to me?'

Monroe was a little patronising. 'Bloody hell, we've got to spoon-feed you now, have we? Alright, but you make sure you let me know pronto if you come up with anything.'

There was further ego-massaging as the conversation ended.

Buoyed by his progress with Monroe, he

rang Harrods and asked to speak to Hopkins, the dapper little man who he had first met at the sushi bar. After several intermediaries, he was put through to Hopkins.

'Mr Hopkins, I am the man who was supposed to meet with Sulamain Khan the day after he was murdered, but as I'm sure you remember, the police accompanied you into the office when you brought me coffee.'

The dapper man appeared anxious and was guarded in his response. 'I was just acting on instructions and don't know anything about the murder. I thought you were taken away for questioning.'

'I was,' he replied. 'But they released me the same evening.'

'Oh, that's good. Why are you ringing me?'

'Actually, I'm involved on the periphery of the investigation and would like to come and see you for a few minutes of your time. Is that's alright?'

Hopkins was dismissive. 'I don't think that would be possible. I'd have to clear it all with my boss and even Mr Al-Fayed, and they're both away at the moment.'

The Gent played his ace card. 'You'll

remember Chief Inspector Monroe, won't you? I'll stay on hold if you wish to call him.'

'Yes, I'm afraid I will have to clear such a sensitive situation. I'll make the call now.'

Ten minutes later, Hopkins was back. 'Yes, I've spoken to Monroe and I'm instructed to afford you all due cooperation.'

'Excellent, I'll be there in half an hour.'

After checking with Jenny, who advised him that Shakira's landline and mobile phone were on voicemail, he was on his way.

His reception this time was more befitting of Harrods, conducted in a brightly decorated office overlooking Knightsbridge. Seated in one of six comfortable leather club chairs placed around a highly polished, expensive looking table, he was served Harrods own-brand coffee and biscuits.

Hopkins was now all civility. 'How may I help you?' he opened.

'Could you tell me what Sulamain's responsibilities were and whether Harrods felt he was performing them as expected?'

Hopkins spouted the party line. 'Mr Sulamain was a highly regarded senior employee, and responsible for all security matters.'

'Could you expand on security matters?'

'Well, in addition to the obvious ones of physical security – locks, windows, doors, outside security patrols – there is liaison with the police in respect of fraud, embezzlement and shoplifting, etc. There are a number of store detectives on duty at any one time. Entrances to the shop have security staff all fully trained in matters of search techniques for weapons or terrorist devices.'

It all sounded good. He tried another question, 'What about deliveries from suppliers?'

'Similar procedures are in place to vet goods received for any tampering with packaging and suppliers are obliged to show ID.'

The Gent enthused, 'It all sounds very comprehensive. What about data security?'

Hopkins's body betrayed the merest hint of unease now. 'I'm not sure what you mean.'

'Did you know Sulamain's wife was a partner in a travel agency business?'

'Yes, I was aware of that.'

'And also that some customers' details were routinely passed over to the agency?'

A shadow of alarm passed over Hopkins's face. 'I had no idea,' he replied.

'Is there anything else you think I need to know?'

Hopkins was relieved that the conversation appeared to be over. 'Nothing at all,' he said.

The Gent decided to leave any questions about the other agency for a future occasion. He rose to leave.

'Well, thank you. I'll let you know if I need anything further.'

On his return, Jenny left no time in describing her success.

'Shakira was all for it,' she announced. 'And we can go round there anytime we want.'

'Excellent, good work. Let's go then. No time like the present. Where is it, by the way?

'She said she would meet us at Putney Bridge Station, and then drive us round to there, if we want to go today.'

Shakira was waiting at the station and walked them round. The agency consisted of a double-fronted shop premises with offices above. There appeared to be four or five staff. Upstairs there were rooms for Shakira and

Latif, and an accounts office, with stores and toilets taking up the remaining space.

At her place of business Shakira seemed to recover a professional veneer, although it was obvious that she was still emotionally fragile. She explained the different functions of each desk. Latif was Relationship Manager for airlines and hotels, with each desk making individual bookings. He also received customer details from Sulamain and marketed travel packages to them either by telesales or e-mail. It all seemed upfront and above board. After coffee they had a chance to talk to Latif on his own in his office, and he confirmed his role as outlined by his mother Shakira.

The Gent put a question to Latif. 'Back at the house, your mother said that any customer data for Sunni pilgrims was generally passed to another agency. Other than the obvious, is there any other reason for this? Are you not losing business by not handling this type of booking?'

Latif's response sounded logical. 'As you can see, we are only a small agency. More investment would be required to handle significant extra business. There would be different airlines and hotel groups to consider, for example.'

He tried a different tack. 'The other agency, which owns them, is it part of a large chain or specialists like this one?'

Latif's answer was measured. 'World Travellers, they are not part of a chain but they are larger than we are.'

He felt there was more. 'Who are the owners, then?'

Latif was still measured. 'I think they are refugees who came over after the wars in the Balkans from Bosnia or one of those places.'

It was not a lot but it was something to stew over.

Jenny, who had remained quiet, suddenly plunged in, 'Latif, how well did you know Samir?'

Latif turned toward Jenny in surprise. 'I haven't seen him in years. I wouldn't say we were very close. He visited a few times when he was down here in London at university, but not really since.'

'You know he worked for your father?'

'No, I didn't,' Latif replied. 'What could he have been doing?'

Jenny glanced at the Gent, who took back control. 'We don't really know, exactly, but that's been very helpful, thanks.'

Feeling enough was enough, they wound up the conversation and briefly re-joined Shakira before heading back to Putney Bridge station and the Tube to Russell Square.

Back in the Imperial, the door had hardly closed before Jenny leapt in, 'Latif is hiding something, I can tell. Isn't he, don't you agree?'

'Yes, I do agree, but what? He was very cagey about the other agency.'

'Let's leave it until the morning and then we'll try Latif again.'

When morning dawned, they decided not to involve Shakira this time, sensing they would get more out of Latif on his own. He said he did not want to worry his mother and agreed to see them again on his own.

The Gent started the ball rolling. 'You were the contact between your father and the agency for customer details.'

'Yes,' Latif said. 'That's correct. Once a month he would give me a printout when I was at the house, and whilst Harrods kind of new, we didn't want any records on e-mail or anything.'

Jenny enquired, 'Did you ever visit your father at work?'

Latif slumped in his chair. 'Yes, I was getting round to telling you. A week or so back I had to go round because the data didn't make sense. It had got corrupted somehow, or the search criteria had been wrongly inputted. The first lines of the address field were in the surname field and email addresses in the postcode field, so I could not do much with it. My father is not – was not – the best at IT skills, so I had to go round and explain. Just as I got there, a man was leaving and I heard him threatening my father.'

'Threatening, you say?' the Gent interjected.

'Yes,' Latif continued. '"Next time or we get you," the man said and ran out towards the lift.'

'Wow!' Jenny exclaimed. 'What happened next?'

'My mother knows nothing of all this,' a relieved Latif said.

They both nodded in agreement.

Latif explained that it had all started when he was approached by World Travellers to become involved in what appeared to be illegal trafficking, as a question was raised by the authorities that a great deal of their incoming business was coming from Eastern Europe rather than *Hajj*-type travel. They'd asked whether Mid East Travel would be interested in taking over some of this surplus. Twelve months earlier, a man from MI6 called Harry Farquarson had asked Latif's father whether he knew anything about this organisation, and he had put Samir onto the case via his friend Will Johnson, who was working there part-time. Both had been casual informants when they had been at Birkbeck College. It was not that difficult, as young overseas students were coming and going as a matter of course, and Mansoor had immediately been suspicious and wanted to find more about it, but without putting Mid East Travel into the firing line. He had asked Samir to update his knowledge.

Latif continued his story from the previous week. 'I challenged my father, and eventually he confessed that he was being blackmailed by the other agency, World Travellers. Ironic, really, when you think about it: blackmail about blackmail! The scam was that they were getting information about potential *Hajj* clients anyway, but wanted extra data and also for other types of Harrods clients so they could be blackmailed or their bank accounts and credit cards hacked. My father categorically refused, and they obviously did get him.'

There was silence as Latif's revelations sank in.

'But he was security,' Jenny said. 'If he'd been warned by them, surely he would have had security stepped up.'

'You're right,' Latif answered. 'And it was. They would never have got past security inside, but they got him in the car park – a knife in the back – and then calmly walked out somehow.'

'What do we do now?' Jenny asked.

The Gent replied, 'I think we have to hand it over to Monroe and his troops now. We've done the hard work. It shouldn't take them long to shake out the actual murderer.'

Monroe was much more amenable this time. 'Morning,' he said cheerfully. 'What have you got for me?'

'An admission from the son Latif: he walked in as Sulamain was being threatened, about a week before the body was found in the car park. Seems this other agency wanted more than a list of potential customers: they were into blackmailing and hacking bank accounts and the like. Call themselves 'World Travellers', and run by Eastern Europeans.'

'Good stuff, well done,' Monroe grudgingly acknowledged. 'Your inside track through Shakira obviously worked. Any proof, though? They're bound to deny all knowledge.'

'Can't be doing all your work for you,' he replied mockingly.

'Suppose not,' Monroe muttered. 'I'm sure we can find some reason to have a look at them. I'll put someone onto it straightaway. And, oh! Thanks.'

Jenny was smiling and looking every inch the Cheshire cat, exclaimed, 'I'm starving. What about we have brunch? I'm not used to working without any breakfast.'

'You're on,' he confirmed, making for the door.

Chapter 26

The next morning, on Friday 29th June, Monroe called before nine o'clock.

'We've got a break: Samir's just phoned. They're in Sainsbury's Whitechapel again, going to have breakfast and then do the shopping. You've met him, haven't you? We need somebody who he knows to pass on some kind of message that we got his call and are now onto them and looking out for him. Think you can do it?'

'Yes, as you know I've met him, so once he sees me he'll realise what we're doing. Have you got a plan of what you need me to do?'

'By the time we pick you up and get there, we will.'

'OK, I'll get down to the car park pronto.'

'Ten minutes at most,' Monroe muttered.

The power of a police vehicle: traffic parted as soon as drivers spied them in the rear-view mirror, and they were there in no time. Parking in a side street invisible from the store, Monroe outlined the plan. New specific details of email and phone numbers were to be passed over, committed to memory, and then disposed of. The house would be under surveillance at all times, and they would be monitored whenever they left the house. If the job was on, he was to run both of his hands twice through his hair as he left the house. In the supermarket, the idea was for him and a female detective to act as Sainsbury-uniformed merchandisers testing a new cheese and biscuits with a small glass of wine if customers wished.

The Gent commented tersely, 'Aren't they supposed to be Muslims? Where does the wine come in?'

Monroe was convincing, 'The intention is to create some kind of a diversion, a conversation, so you can get eye contact with Samir and pass him the note, maybe on the plate as you give it to him.'

'I guess it's almost plausible, though on the hoof as it is. Will the note mention Sulamain? He's bound to be wondering.'

Monroe was thoughtful. 'I haven't got that far.'

'That gives us all of five minutes,' the Gent responded sarcastically.

Monroe looked apologetic. 'I know, I know. Do you think he could handle it? It's a pretty tall order: 'oh, by the way, your uncle's dead, but you just act normal.''

They were certainly in a quandary. If it went wrong, Samir and his friends were for the chop: literally. Time was running out. They looked like they were finishing breakfast.

The Gent went for the diplomatic option. 'We stall, play for time, even if he were able to ask, it would not only put his but many other lives at risk, not to mention the whole operation having to be aborted.'

Monroe was relieved, 'Exactly what I was thinking.' They parked out front and made their way round to the back door, which was already open, where the manager stood waiting with uniforms at the ready. The plan was that because he knew Samir he would approach him first in order to keep him back, while Jenny followed the others to distract them should they stop or turn around. One minute later an undercover female detective and a gentleman walked the floor, entrapping unwary punters with a tray full of free goodies. They saw the group of five Asian men starting down aisle 4, stocking cereals and branded bread, crackers, etc. As they began to turn round into the next aisle, with

Samir at the rear, the Gent picked his moment.

'Good morning, sir. Would you like to try our finest home counties, farm-produced, locally-sourced cheese, with a glass of fine French wine, if it's not too early in the day?'

He prattled on for a minute as the rest of the group turned the corner. There was a startled expression in Samir's eyes, but his composure never wavered. Jenny was behind Samir at the corner, right behind the rest of the group and ready to pounce if they paused or turned. Samir then recognised him. With a shake of his head, a finger to his lips and pointing to the plate, the note was passed, read and committed to memory before the cheese was eaten. At the point he heard his colleague speak.

'Good morning, gentlemen. Would you like to try our finest?'

Time was up.

Samir almost hammed it up, 'That was delightful. I must buy some next time I visit, and yes, it is too early in the day for alcohol, but thanks very much.'

Mission accomplished.

They carried on accosting unwitting

shoppers for a few minutes, actually making two sales, which impressed the manager. The group meanwhile pottered around shopping for another half hour.

Back in the car there was a debriefing. Monroe was pleased at the result. Monroe was in the mood to talk further, but it would be easier to go back to Kensington police station and drop off the other police officers.

As they were driving away, the group were leaving the store unobserved by all in the police Vauxhall Insignia. The reverse applied to the exiting shoppers: all occupants of the vehicle were visible to the group, none more so than Patterson sat in the rear, which was immediately recognised by Tariq the minder with the nasty streak and a fondness for Samir. He also instantly recognised the man sat next to Patterson as the same man trying to sell wine to Samir forty-five minutes earlier in the supermarket. Something was dreadfully wrong, but what? He couldn't figure it at out at first. And then it struck him: Patterson was the man he had seen in a Vauxhall Insignia some yards down the street from the safe house using a mobile and checking a map as if trying to locate a particular property. It was obvious to Tariq that Patterson was a policeman, and the other man, was he a policeman too? Then he remembered that face from somewhere else... yes, the British Museum, where he had been assigned to stalk Samir on his fact-finding mission some weeks earlier. Samir had been with a blonde girl, but when they separated he knew Samir would be some time in his Islamic research so he opted to follow the girl. His instincts proved correct when he spotted her in animated conversation with this very same man sat alongside Patterson in the police Vauxhall Insignia.

Tariq pulled Hussein to one side and quickly explained his observations. Hussein thought for a moment and then commanded, 'Take the car and follow them. They will go back to the police station. When he leaves, see where he goes from there. Keep me informed. We'll soon know if he is with the Met or not.'

Tariq took off after the police car whilst Hussein and the rest of the group hailed a taxi.

The Gent was pleased to be entertained at Kensington police station in less formal circumstances than those of his first visit.

The debriefing had only taken a short time, but on leaving the police station he had that strange feeling of eyes watching him as he hailed a cab to take him back to the hotel.

Meanwhile, back at the safe house, Samir was both excited and relieved that someone was at last looking out for him, but quite why it was the friend of Jenny's from Bannerman's club he had no idea. He guessed he must be something to do with the police, as must his female colleague from the supermarket.

Later on that day, the group went to Friday prayers. It was like a day out, for the venue was the London Central Mosque in Regents Park, where Ibrahim Abelgadar was visiting. The mosque was huge, capable of holding five thousand worshippers, and was part of the Islamic Cultural Centre. It was originally founded during World War II, in recognition of the substantial Muslim population of the British Empire and its support for the Allies during World War II. Just across the outer circle road of Regent's Park is Winfield House and grounds, the US Ambassador's official residence. Ambassador Susman is host to a popular event each year the fourth July picnic in the grounds to celebrate American Independence Day.

Afterwards, in a back room, the group,

along with Hussein, with whom there was now a definite bonding, met with Abelgadar. 'The time for *jihad* is upon us,' he raged to a delighted following. 'The will of Allah shall prevail. You are all heroes, soldiers of Islam.' The time would be in the next week he said; preparations were being made. They would be told their roles soon.

Ibrahim Abelgadar finished his prayers. He was a happy man, content that Allah was on his side. The group were now ready: Hussein had prepared them well. He fully approved their vengeance against whoremongers, violators of children, and, whilst not exactly in line with Sharia law, he knew Allah would approve of his soldiers having to make courageous decisions in the heat of battle. English justice was too weak and would take too long anyhow.

He was calm now; the time was ripe. On the surface, Ibrahim was an old-fashioned cleric, but he was prepared to embrace technology in the work of Allah. His BlackBerry dinged. He picked it up, answering slowly, not expecting a call. It was his father.

'Ibrahim, my son, how are you? What is the situation on our mission?'

'I am fine, my father. We are prepared for your mission, one of many I must perform before I leave this land of infidels and nonbelievers. Do not worry, you will be truly avenged and your enemies taught a lesson they will not forget.'

His father was pleased. 'You will let me know.'

Ibrahim replied, 'Keep your eyes on the news channels. You will see soon enough. I have to go; they will be tracking this call. I must move quickly.'

'Thank you, my son. Allah is praised.'

Ibrahim recalled the days when his family had been wealthy. Shia Muslims, they had travelled throughout the Middle East from Iraq to Syria to Bahrain, where Ibrahim's father was caught up in the political unrest of recent years between Bahrain and neighbouring states. They had been imprisoned without trial, and all their wealth was lost. The vengeance in their hearts was intolerable: only the blood of their enemies would remove this burden.

Tariq was getting impatient as he kept watch on the police station from two-hundred yards down the road, pretending to be a private hire car driver on his mobile. He could only keep this up for a short period of time. It would be too dangerous to stay for long. He need not have worried: the Gent emerged after about twenty minutes, looking up and down the street for a black cab. One appeared almost immediately. Tariq had actually been a private hire driver and had no trouble keeping several vehicles behind the Hackney cab.

The Gent alighted and went through the archway into the Imperial Hotel. Tariq drove on around Russell Square and found a place to park. *What next?* He thought. *Not the usual abode of a Met policeman.* He phoned Hussein, but it went to voicemail. Now what? He could hardly enter the hotel dressed as he was and with several days' growth of heavy dark beard. He was not exactly your typical Imperial client.

The mobile interrupted his thoughts. It was Hussein.

'Hello, yes,' he answered. 'The man took a cab from the police station to the Imperial Hotel in Russell Square. I'm parked up around the corner.'

'Well done, my brother,' Hussein praised him. 'You'll have to go in and sort him out. Find out who he is and what he is doing.'

Tariq was reticent. 'But I am on my own and will look obviously out of place as I am, with beard.'

Hussein became angry. 'Idiot, I will send

someone to assist. He can watch while you go and change.'

Twenty minutes later, Mustapha arrived, suited and clean-shaven.

Another half hour and Tariq was back after his own transformation: at a casual glance they could have been out-of-town salesmen, but for Marks & Spencer £50 suits, the effect belying their cost.

Sitting in Tariq's ancient Nissan Almera, a problem was quickly identified: they had neither name nor room number, and only Tariq had eyeball. Everyone needed a stroke of luck, and every man needed to eat. It was lunchtime. Their strategy: to affect a meeting over coffee and biscuits in the hotel lobby, where they could observe reception and lifts. Allah was bountiful, and after an hour their patience was rewarded: the target came out of the ground-floor restaurant and headed for the lifts. Mustapha, who could never have been seen by the man, quickly followed. Mustapha was last to alight from the lift. Looking around as if in doubt; he watched the target enter a room halfway down the corridor. He strolled past to the end, noting the number. He was back sitting with Tariq ten minutes later.

Grinning broadly, he said, 'Room 425 on the fourth floor.'

'Right, let's go,' Tariq commanded.

The Gent was dozing after his solitary lunch. Jenny was not yet back from her trip to Waterstones book shop on Gower Street. A knock on the door roused him. He stumbled over to the door. Expecting Jenny, he realised he had not heard her voice.

'Hello, Jenny?' he enquired.

'No, sir, towels,' a voice answered.

He opened the door and a large fist smacked him right between the eyes. As he stepped back, another followed, doubling him up as a third crashed into the side of his head, buckling his legs like a prize-fighter going down from the knock-out punch. Minutes later, his head was still hurting and the television was on. He was tied to chair with a gag in his mouth, and two large Asian men were standing menacingly over him. Inwardly, he cursed himself for making it so easy. Time was he would have dealt with both in singular fashion, but that was a long time ago.

One man seemed to be in charge. The other threw water in his face to wake him up. He

259

worried about Jenny, who would be due back by now. The man in charge spoke, 'You are in serious trouble. We have to find out why you are spying on us. We have very little time. If you do not cooperate, my friend will kill you.'

Experience told him that in situations like this it was better to tell as much of the truth as possible in order not to be caught out. He didn't get the opportunity, as the other man hit him again and he fainted. Coming round a moment later, he tried to explain.

'I'm only helping to find a man who has gone missing. Samir Khan, His family are very worried.'

In-charge man spoke, 'You already know Samir. We saw you in the supermarket.' To the other man, he barked, 'Get the wet towel.'

He knew what was coming, and instantly he was sweating. *Mustn't panic*, he thought, as the towel was placed over his mouth and nose. It was too late. He thrashed about and tried to jerk his head, but they were too strong. He was losing consciousness. He kept struggling, and the panic was there now. He was back in *that place*. The uniforms were laughing; he was surely going to die this time...

In his unconscious state he regressed. If he died now, what would happen to his wife

Mary and daughter Sam? He would have to fight it, get through it somehow. His mind went back to Sandhurst: the marathon training runs up the hills when your mind is not your own and it becomes blank. Endorphins kick in, you can't feel your legs, but somehow they keep pumping and you get through *the wall*; over the top, running downhill. And then, something else was happening: he was on a train. It was labouring up a steep incline. Now it was coming into a station – it wasn't stopping! It would hit the buffers at speed. Oh! My God, this is it. C*rash!*

No crash! He was waking up, breathing fast and heavy. He was alive!

Jenny was pleased as she skipped along Gower Street on her way back from Waterstones to the hotel. She had made several purchases: two more cookery books for Mother, a Mills and Boon for Granny and a get-fit-in-a-week book for herself. It was a bright day, so she detoured through Russell Square Park, taking in the sun and wondering what the rest of the afternoon and evening had in store. She hoped he had booked the Italian restaurant again; the last time had been wonderful. The lobby of the Imperial Hotel was busy. It was the time of year for overseas tourists. She had to wait ten minutes for the lift to the fourth floor.

She knocked on the door to room number 425.

'It's me!' she cried. 'Hello?' There was no answer. He must be in, as he would have texted if he was going out.

She rapped on the door and tried again.

'Hello, hello, are you there?'

The door was suddenly yanked open and a large Asian-looking man grabbed her arm. Looking into the room, the vanity mirror on the wall above the writing bureau gave her a view of the horrific scene taking place in the room. She shrieked, and that and the instinctive sharp kick to the shins of the assailant was enough for his grip to loosen and enable her to wrestle herself away. She ran screaming down the corridor.

'Help, help, he's dead! They've killed him,' she cried, 'Police!'

Doors opened, and people alighting from the lift stared, transfixed. One man realised the drama unfolding and grabbed her by both arms.

'Stop, stop!' he shouted. 'Which room?'

'Back there, back there!' Jenny stammered.

The man propelled her along the corridor to the room just as Tariq and Mustapha burst out and ran off in the other direction towards the stairs.

The scene in the room was not good: the Gent was definitely back in *that place*. The wet towel had slipped from his face, which was bloodied and bruised. He was barely conscious, sweating profusely and shaking.

He muttered, 'All I know, all I know. Sleep. Please let me sleep now.'

Jenny wept as she tenderly wrapped her arms around his head. The man from the lift removed the belts used to tie him to the chair.

'It's OK now,' she whispered as he slowly came out of his nightmare.

The man opened the fridge and poured two drinks.

Handing each of them a brandy, he said, 'My name's John Forbes. I'm a medical rep from Gloucester. I think you both need this. What on earth is happening? It looks a bit strong for a cash mugging.'

Jenny took a large slug of her brandy before attempting to reply. 'Yes, you're right, but I'm not sure I can tell you.'

There was a burp as the Gent finished off his brandy and asked for another. He would have looked a bit like a footballer after the magic sponge was it not for the caked blood and bruises. He was clearly still in shock, but the effect of the brandy was remarkable. Just then the assistant manager ran into the room.

'What on earth is happening?' he said.

'I've been mugged,' the Gent quickly replied, before Jenny or John Forbes could speak.

Forbes advised, 'You clearly need some attention. I am not a doctor, but I did go to medical school, although I kept fainting in the operating theatre. Here, let me have a quick look at you before I have to go.'

He speedily dabbed at the facial contusions with a damp cloth and checked the bruises. He was relieved that standing did not appear to be a problem, and concluded, 'You've been very lucky. You might have a headache, but nothing seems to be broken. However, I would suggest you get checked out by a doctor. I'll be off now. Let me know if I can help further, statement to the police or anything, you know. Good luck.'

'I'll get the police.' the manager offered when Forbes had gone.

'That's OK,' Jenny insisted. 'We've already been in contact and someone is on the way.'

'Oh, right,' he remarked, unconvinced. 'We do have a member of staff trained in health and safety. I'll send her up with some painkillers, paracetamol or something. Well, you know where I am if you need me,' he added, leaving the room.

There was a joint sigh as the door closed, allowing them to try and figure out their next move.

'Ahem,' Jenny uttered. 'You were in a bit of a state before, as though you thought you were somewhere else. Do you want to tell me about it?'

'Yes, you're right. I will explain, but now is not the time. We need to think and get in touch with Monroe and Spinner.'

A minute later there was a knock at the door; the health and safety lady must have sprinted all the way. Duly fussed over and plied with painkillers and hot, sweet, tea, which would normally have tasted foul, he started to feel better despite having to sign the hotel's disclaimer form about not going to hospital.

Chapter 27

It was a surprise when two days later his mobile rang and it was Will Johnson. He had not expected Will to return the call, having moved out of London and now living in Brighton.

Glancing up at Jenny, he quickly gathered his thoughts and explained, 'Will, thanks for getting back to me. I am working on behalf of Samir's parents. He seems to have gone missing, and they are obviously anxious as to his whereabouts. He went down to London a couple of weeks ago and has not been in touch, nor has he been back to work. I've tried Brian Foster, another old friend, but he has not heard from Samir for at least a couple of months.'

Will's response appeared guarded. Was he onto something? 'Yes, I was at Birkbeck with Samir and Brian. Samir and I were good friends. Brian was not quite as close. I've heard what you said, but how do I know I can trust you?'

'Well, you don't, but I would be happy to come down to Brighton and meet you.'

'No, there's no need for that. I could come up to London. It's a regular trip for me anyway.'

The response was immediate; he tried a more probing question. 'Why did you move to London?'

'That's personal.' Will responded defensively, he was definitely onto something now.

'I could meet you tomorrow, if you like. I've nothing urgent on at the moment, and I commute to London and back to Brighton on a regular basis.'

'I'm staying at the Imperial Hotel in Russell Square. Is that OK?'

'Yes sure. If I leave first thing I could be there for say ten, something like that.'

'Yes, that would be fine. See you in the morning, then.'

Will Johnson arrived at five minutes to ten the next morning, casually dressed but smart in a dark suit with open-necked white shirt. He had an Adriatic look about him: about six feet tall and athletic-looking, and could easily have been a soccer player or tennis pro with a name ending in Ivanovic, or similar.

Gesturing for Will to be seated, the Gent introduced Jenny as his colleague and offered coffee and warm croissants, which were accepted with enthusiasm. He felt it obligatory to open the discussion.

'Thank you for taking the trouble to come all the way from Brighton. Perhaps I could first explain our involvement in the situation.'

Will's body language exhibited signs of distrust. Responding cautiously, he said, 'Yes, I would appreciate that, but what happened to your face?'

'I was mugged,' he explained, matter-of-factly.

Without going into the intricate details of credit cards, etc., he briefly summarised Jenny's relationship with Samir: their knowing each other via Forest View Golf Club, and her request for advice. Leaving out the intricate details of the police, MI6 and the Met, he outlined their meetings with Shakira and her request for help in the search for Samir.

'We have had to talk to the Met to advise them of a missing person scenario. They, of course, would prefer if we amateurs left them to it, but there you are. Your name came from discussion with Samir's parents, who are now seriously worried, as you would expect.'

Will's demeanour visibly changed, and he became more relaxed as he began to speak. 'That's explains a lot. You know, Samir and I go back a long way, to our time in university at Birkbeck College.'

'Yes, we do know that.' More hesitantly, Will volunteered, 'Are you also aware that his uncle Sulamain is an ex-Met policeman and is in security at Harrods?'

There were anxious glances. Will was obviously not aware of Sulamain's demise. The answer came from Jenny, 'Yes, Samir did tell me about him.'

Will settled himself in his chair and prepared to relate his story. 'Well, going right back to our college days, Samir, Bill and me first became mates after a heavy session in the bar, where a unanimous decision the morning after confirmed we needed to do something to keep fit. It was Brian's idea really, He was much taller and heavier and was in the pack for the second eleven of the Rugby Union team; he had ambitions for the first eleven but needed to become more mobile. I had been athletic at school, as had Samir, mainly cross-country running. Samir was also a runner and a soccer player, and his stamina gained from the demands of cross-country made him a natural for midfield. I can't quite remember why now, but we ended up doing kick-boxing and I believe Samir still keeps in shape at a local class held in an old mill in downtown Stockport.

'He was recruited on a part-time basis to report to his uncle on any strange goings-on at university in terms of potential terrorist activity. There are always political debates and people going to sort out the establishment and what have you, and most of it turns out to be bullshit, if you will excuse the expression. But occasionally there were serious intentions, and we would take note, and if we thought necessary pass it on to Sulamain.'

The Gent interjected, 'You say 'we'…'

'Yes, that's right.' Will confirmed. 'We were best of friends, and I just kind of fell into it. Being involved in the student union, helping out with travel arrangements and stuff like that, we got to know most of the new overseas arrivals. We also used to work for a travel agency sometimes during holidays. There were one or two dodgy practices going on there, which we passed on to Sulamain.'

'What was the name of the agency, by the way?'

'World Travellers, they do a lot of *Hajj* work.'

He and Jenny were both suddenly on full alert. 'What kind of practices made you suspicious?' the Gent asked.

'Well, at one time we were convinced that they were bringing illegals into the country and possibly sending others out as well.'

'What evidence was there for you to reach such a conclusion?'

'There were occasions from time to time where groups of five or six would come in to the agency, usually accompanied by the same guy. They would always go to an upstairs office for a while. When they left the office, they all had large envelopes, as though they had collected lots of documents. One time we went upstairs when they had gone, and there was a file that had been left on the desk. The man must have forgotten to file it away. It contained passports and driving licences. Whenever we overheard conversations, the people could not speak English very well.'

'What happened after this information was passed on to Sulamain?'

'I don't really know. When we finished university, we stopped this work. And I lost touch a bit with Samir. Then about a year ago I was made redundant and needed money, so I contacted them again and they gave me some part-time work.'

'Was Samir aware of this?'

'Yes, he was. He came down from time to time and he had been asked by his uncle to try and get back in there, but obviously it would be difficult as he was ostensibly still based up North, so basically I acted for him.'

'So what is the situation now?'

'I now have a job working for an advertising agency with an office in the City and also one in Brighton. I've been concerned about Samir for some weeks now, and when the bloke from World Travellers came round and threatened me with a knife because they knew I had been snooping, I put two and two together and decided it might be healthier if I stopped working there altogether and based myself in Brighton.'

There was a dual "Wow!" in response, and the Gent added, 'That's quite a story, Will, and it certainly explains a lot and makes a few pieces fit together.'

After promising to keep him informed, a much relieved Will left for his London office.

Chief Inspector Monroe and Detective Sergeant Patterson were on a stake- out, watching the safe house. They had observed the group return from shopping at Sainsbury's. The group had become trusted, and it was now taken as normal for them to perform the routine shop at Sainsbury's. This and Samir's newly acquired bladder infection allowed him to visit Sainsbury's facilities without suspicion and of course for him to covertly use the telephone situated in the corridor.

The minder came back out quickly, catching them unawares as they were about to drive off. By parking the car facing towards them, he had them wrong-footed and drove off at speed, leaving it necessary for them to turn around, by which time they'd lost him.

'Bollocks!' cursed Patterson, slamming his fist onto the dash.

'Keep driving!' shouted Monroe. 'I'll get the other two cars to keep a look-out. There are only two directions he can go from here to reach main roads, so fingers crossed we'll spot him in five minutes. Otherwise it's back to square one until he returns... whatever; he's got something to hide.'

They were lucky, courtesy of a pallet truck that had shed its load. The Polish driver had been unable to read a one-way street sign, and narrowly avoiding an oncoming black cab, the front end was now stuck in the window of a fruit and veg shop, the outside wooden tables broken with contents strewn over the pavement. All traffic was at a standstill for several streets around. The minder sprinted away, leaving the driver's door wide open and the engine still running, but was soon apprehended by an athletic female police constable.

Back at Kensington police station, he was taken to a room for questioning. He wore a creased traditional pyjama-style *shalwar kameez* with a stained black waistcoat, giving his name as Mustapha Iqbal. He spoke passable English, but was unable to provide further identification, saying he was from Birmingham looking for work, the address still to be checked. Monroe was called away, leaving further interrogation to Patterson.

Patterson, assisted by a police constable, pressed on. 'Mr Iqbal, can you explain why you ran out of the car and drove off at high speed?'

Nervous and fidgety, Iqbal's reply was not convincing. 'I forget things from shop.'

'What kind of things, Mr Iqbal? We know you had just returned from Sainsbury's, but what could be so urgent as to require such speed? We can easily check what is in the house.'

The eyes had it now, darting all around the room as if for inspiration, and then it dawned on him how to buy time. 'I not understand, need interpreter.'

Patterson was not unduly surprised. 'That could take some time. It might be tomorrow before one is available.'

Iqbal tried another tack, 'I am hungry, need food.'

Patterson played along, 'Yes, you can have some water, but it's not time to serve food for another three hours. Can you give me the name of somebody who can vouch for you, and also confirm the veracity of your statement? That you are temporarily in residence at that address you drove away from?'

Iqbal's understanding suddenly improved now that he was not under any immediate threat. 'Yes, yes, Imam Hassani from local mosque.'

Patterson was relieved. He did not want to prejudice the stake-out by having to enter the house, and it was obvious that Iqbal did not really need an interpreter. The next move would be up to Monroe.

He left the room to consult Monroe.

'What do you think then, sir?' Patterson asked.

'Well done,' praised Monroe, uncharacteristically. 'He definitely does not want us in that house for some reason. Get someone round to the mosque and see if they've heard of him, then I think we'll have another word with him.'

As expected, the local imam confirmed Iqbal's story.

Back in the interrogation room, Monroe had some questions.

'Mr Iqbal, Imam Hassani has confirmed he knows you. You said earlier that you drove off at speed to get back to Sainsbury's. When we found you stuck in traffic, you were headed in the wrong direction. Can you explain that?'

The eyes again, he was cornered, 'I thought you were chasing me,' he said.

'And why should we do that, Mr Iqbal?'

'I not mean you, police Mr Monroe. Others,' Iqbal stammered.

Monroe was confident they were onto something now. 'What others Mr Iqbal?'

'Yes, well, I do work for some people,

getting people into country, explain things, you know,' Iqbal prattled on.

'Yes, I believe I do know,' Patterson said. 'So why are you afraid of these others?'

Iqbal was all for getting it off his chest. 'They are bad men from Eastern Europe. Sometimes they bring in children and girls, sell them to gangs, you know, even English white girls, one time they bring girls back to the house and there was a big fight. Hussein did not like it, he goes mad and we had to move.'

Monroe was most curious. 'So do they have a name? They must have some kind of cover. Do they have normal customers as a front?'

Iqbal let it out. 'I don't know for sure, only that people at the agency talk about how a Mr Sulamain is very good for them.'

Monroe and Patterson were flabbergasted, but remained calm. Patterson allowed Monroe to continue. 'And who is Mr Sulamain?'

Iqbal looked finished. 'I don't know, honestly, I don't know any more.'

Patterson was obliging, 'We'll let the imam know you are here, Mr Iqbal. It might the safest place for a day or two.'

Monroe and Patterson left the room.

'What do you think, boss?' Patterson wondered.

'I don't think Iqbal is the biggest villain in all this. He knows more than he is saying, but basically he's just a hired hand. Let's keep him around for a bit, and maybe something else will slip or his memory will improve.'

Chapter 28

Jenny and the Gent were in the Atrium coffee shop at the Imperial, trying to figure out where they were headed. He was convinced that the other agency was somehow involved in the murder of Sulamain; it was too much of a coincidence. They ordered coffee and French croissants, perfect elevenses.

His mobile rang. It was Monroe. 'That meeting with Spinner, he wants it in the morning. Is that OK?'

The question seemed absurd in the circumstances, but he thought better than to say so. 'Yes, no problem.'

'Spinner thinks it best if we come over there, better for you not to have your face all over the CCTV cameras.'

'Yes, OK.'

'See you about ten thirty, then. Oh, and you can include the girl if you want.'

The Gent was perturbed at first. Why was there a tail on him? But Monroe was a policeman, after all. Ah! They would have been watching the house of Shakira Khan in Wimbledon. Jenny looked at him quizzically.

'Is there something wrong?'

He explained the misunderstanding as the coffee and croissants arrived.

They skipped lunch, settling for afternoon tea, where they discussed their plans for the meeting the next day. What plans? Apart from his theories, which would appear fanciful, to hardened policemen there was still not enough to determine a target.

Saturday evening, a nice evening in London, would be too good an opportunity to waste. He reserved a table at Ciao Bella in Bloomsbury, where they had previously dined. The weather was perfect, with a bright orange sun setting over Russell Square. Looking the part, she was in white linen trousers and an azure top with shoestring straps, and he was in a blue-striped short-sleeved shirt and Ted Baker charcoal slacks. They strolled together over to the restaurant.

The maître d' welcomed them as only Italians can, and his riposte of remembering them was almost convincing. The restaurant was situated over two floors: a bright and buzzy ground floor and a more relaxed and intimate basement. They opted for Bombay

Sapphire gin and tonics with ice and lime, and the live piano played as they perused the menu. From the chef's special menu, Jenny chose asparagus olande, followed by fegati and bacon; while his choice was involtini di salmone con avocado with a main course of tagliata di manzo. The waiter recommended a bottle of Montepulciano Riveria Aldiano (2007).

They discussed a host of things. Jenny offloaded about her grandmother, and the world and its problems were all sorted out. They were even convinced their golf had improved. The events that had led them to be there in the first place were also somehow forgotten. Their own relationship was never mentioned. To the waiter, however, they were clearly... well, you know.

Strolling back, there was no need to talk. It was dusk, and arm in arm they walked through the gardens in Russell Square. In a secluded spot, they embraced. He kissed her passionately, and her response was equal. As they gazed at each other, their eyes spoke the truth as pure as mountain dew. They walked a few steps and Jenny stopped and asked him.

'Why have you never made a pass at me?'

'It's not because I don't... you know.'

He floundered for a moment and went on

to explain in detail about Sheila and the tragic circumstances of her death only weeks before.

She embraced him again. 'I never realised, I never knew, I am so sorry.'

They walked back to the hotel in silence.

On entering the reception area, he said, 'It's still quite early. Would you like—'

He never finished the sentence. The alarms went off and panic reigned. An elderly man stood up from his table, pint glass of beer in hand, staggered a few paces and collapsed into the lap of a heavily made-up buxom lady, knocking over that table and spilling drinks over those gathered around it. The hotel staff were scurrying about, ushering guests out of the hotel and over the street back into the gardens of Russell Square, from whence they had come only minutes before.

Sirens screamed as police and fire-tenders made their way over. The streets around became jammed with traffic as police prevented vehicles going anywhere near the hotel for the time being. Three hours later, the hotel staff led the now shivering guests back. It had been a false alarm. The rumblings of dissent were quelled by free coffee and drinks, but it was another hour before normalcy returned and guests were able to retire to their rooms. With a resigned look and a wistful wave, the Gent bade Jenny good night.

It was Sunday morning, 1st July. They met for breakfast, both soberly attired as befitting their meeting later that morning. Afterwards, they quietly discussed how the proceedings might play out.

Spinner arrived first, and Jenny was introduced and the reason for her presence explained to Spinner, who was not at all concerned. Monroe and Patterson arrived late, cursing about how much of a problem the previous night's events had been for the Met, and all for a false alarm.

Spinner took the floor. 'Good morning, gentlemen and Ms Lomas. As you know we have been scheduled to meet for some time now, in order to disseminate the information we all variously hold about what started out as a relatively low-level alert about a potential terrorist plot emanating from Manchester, begun by the brave action of Ms Lomas. This has since escalated into what we now know as the Sword of Allah events, one in Manchester and a similar one here in London, although no one was killed in that event. Samir, as you know, has been acting as an undercover agent, originally on a small basis, funnelling information through his uncle, Sulamain Khan, who was my agent. I don't need to tell you that Samir is now an agent in the full sense of the word, and in extreme danger. Even though there is a bonding in the original group, I am including the man known as Hussein here: they would have no hesitation in killing him for their cause.'

Monroe interjected, 'Do we know precisely what that cause is?'

Spinner continued, 'That's the crux of the problem. The perpetrators – let's call them foot-soldiers – are motivated by idealism. The planners and strategists could be acting for a number of reasons, including pure Islamic fundamentalism, Nationalism or personal vendetta. I attended a meeting this morning at MI5 where a whole host of issues were discussed. A GMP report written by Inspector Bill Lambert was circulated, with a surprising lack of comment about this particular matter. It seems that on that score certainly they have gone to ground in Manchester, although there was reference to a local group of idiots calling themselves KNI, who were throwing petrol bombs through the windows of the Etihad Stadium. The perpetrators were quickly apprehended, and they confessed to being paid, but who was paying them is not yet known.'

It was Monroe's turn again. 'We had a lucky break. When we arrested a minder from the safe house, who was also moonlighting for a travel agency, said he was doing interpretation for immigrants. He'd been threatened by an Eastern European gang for trying to muscle in on their territory. When they asked him where his agency got customers from, guess what came up? The name of a man called Sulamain.'

Spinner turned to the Gent and said, 'You're the analyst. What's your take on it all?'

He spoke thoughtfully. 'Well, as you know, I got involved quite early on in this scenario, through Jenny. I never perceived Samir as a terrorist in the first place, and my impression after meeting him was that on his part there was something more going on than fundamental Islamic ideology, but can we concentrate on Sulamain first because we may be able to close this one. As you know, we have been working for Samir's parents and Sulamain's widow Shakira specifically on the whereabouts of Samir. We have talked to Shakira and her son Latif and visited their travel agency, where we gained a great deal of information, not least that another agency, called World Travellers, are into some very dodgy practices, and it's they who I'll bet are the outfit threatening Iqbal. We have also

285

managed to trace two old college friends of Samir, a Will Johnson and Brian Foster. The latter was not able to tell us much, but Will confirmed that he and Samir have been passing information onto Sulamain for years. In fact, they both at various times have worked part time at World Travellers, and Will has also been threatened by them, sufficiently so to up sticks to Brighton.'

He went on explain in detail about the assorted nefarious activities in which World Travellers were involved.

Spinner was impressed. 'By golly, you two have been busy!'

Monroe, though less enthused, was also complimentary. 'I can only agree, and you have certainly saved me a whole lot of work.'

Jenny was all smiles at the compliments, while the Gent continued relating his views on the terrorist plot.

'Getting back to the plotters then, thinking about it, I couldn't understand what they would achieve by targeting the British Museum, unless it was purely a demonstration of power. If that were the case, it could have been done in Manchester or in any public place in London, although the capital would have more kudos. The Jubilee celebrations have been and gone, and the Olympics are still weeks away, so if something is planned it has to be soon. I do have a few thoughts about whom and why, which I'd like to share...'

Before he could continue, Monroe's pager went off. He needed to ring in immediately. He left the meeting but quickly returned.

'We've had a telephone call from Samir. It is going to happen this week, but he doesn't know what the target is yet.'

The Gent was first to respond. 'How are we going to communicate with Samir?'

Monroe answered, 'the house is being watched 24/7. The plan is to catch them in the act before it actually happens. The difficulty is, there is nothing physical in the house that is incriminating, and by that I mean bomb-making equipment, firearms and the like, so we can only assume they would pick it up on the way or be met at the target.'

Spinner was right back. 'Yes, it is being watched 24/7, but it depends on what they plan to do. The assumption is always some kind of bomb to kill as many people as possible, but they are getting more sophisticated, with more assassinations and kidnappings.'

Jenny then commented, 'So what you're saying is that in many other instances the equipment and personnel are all there in the one house and you can just walk in and arrest them?'

Monroe countered, 'It isn't usually quite so simple, but in essence you're on the right track. What we've got here, notwithstanding the Sword of Allah issue, is that we have potential perpetrators only in the house and nothing else. I've only got leeway on the Sword of Allah issue because it is believed something much, much bigger is being planned, and to get a conviction we need to catch them in the act or at least just before the act with enough hard evidence to commit an act in their possession.'

Spinner, who had evidently designated himself chairman of the meeting, turned again to the Gent. 'You were about to say something a minute or so ago before Monroe's pager went off.'

'Oh yes, I was, but first do we know any more about Ibrahim Abelgadar? He seems to be the one pulling the strings. Does he have a family here? Is he claiming benefits, that kind of thing? Can we build up any kind of history for him? He can't have turned up out of thin air. Does he have any old associates in the country?'

Spinner looked at Monroe and he nodded for the MI6 man to speak.

'We know from our overseas agents that he hails from Baghdad, where they began various business ventures, but owing to the numerous troubles and wars – Saddam Hussein, etc. – the family travelled and ended up in Bahrain. Out of the frying pan and into the fire, so to speak, for during the political unrest there in Bahrain in recent years, Ibrahim and his father were not favourites of the establishment and ended up being imprisoned and tortured. Their bank accounts were frozen and assets confiscated, all the wealth of the family lost. As foreigners they were unable to identify individuals plotting against them, putting the blame on Sunni Muslims for their plight. Most of the family returned to Iraq, and Abelgadar came to Britain, where his front is that of firebrand cleric, but we think there is more.'

Spinner turned to the Gent. 'Is that helpful in your analysis?'

'Yes, it is. The trio, apart from Samir who we now know is an agent, are idealists and appear to be able and willing to carry this off, especially with Hussein involved. I have been doing a fair bit of research, and this doesn't feel like the July 7th London bombings or a shoe-bomber scenario where the perpetrators are like lone wolves on a suicide mission sent out to bomb indiscriminate targets. The fact that Abelgadar is staying involved and that

Hussein is very much leading things on the ground suggests that they have been kept together and will stick together throughout the assignment.'

Monroe joined in, 'You could have something there. As I said before, there is no equipment in the house, and all the other occupants, even if they are illegals, could ostensibly be looking for work.'

Spinner summed up, 'Well, it seems we broadly agree that something is up and going to happen very soon. I think we are dependent very much on your surveillance team, Inspector, to shout when there is any sign of movement from the house, unless Samir can get us any more information.'

All agreed to be ready for the call.

Chapter 29

Life in the house was pretty much routine – boring, in fact – despite knowing the call was imminent. Even Samir was bored; it was impossible to be on red-alert 24/7. When they were not playing chess, Ali and Abdullah spent hours sermonising and debating the depravity of the West and justifying the actions they were going to take to save the world. They could have been hippies from the sixties, except that bombs got you more attention than lying down in the street with a bunch of flowers. Got you dead, in fact!

Samir wondered why they couldn't just twit and tweet, or even be hackers, but then Julian Assange, founder of Wikileaks, had fallen foul of the US authorities, hadn't he? The barking duo was still barking: Ahmed and Jubail had been accepted by G4S and were to begin their training the following week.

Ali had raised questions after their last sermon from Abelgadar.

'Do you think we will be given any weapons, sub-machines guns or grenades?'

Samir countered, 'It's not a game on your

291

Sony PlayStation, you idiot.'

Abdullah concurred. 'Don't be daft, Ali, you know whatever is needed will be provided at the time. We only have to place it where instructed and we know Hussein will be with us.'

'Yeah, that's what worries me,' Ali fired back, ending the debate.

Samir's head was in turmoil. He was remorseful, doubtful, and he had turned on his friends. Yes, they were wrong, but strangely immature, believing what they were told without question by the imam and Hussein, who was the biggest loose cannon you could ever imagine. He anguished about how he was going to get the word out to the police, or that man, Jenny's friend, (who the hell he was, anyway), unless he could get to Sainsbury's again. He reasoned that they must be watching the place, so if an opportunity did not occur and word came that they were off, then they would be tailed. He hoped they were good at that job, otherwise the whole thing could be aborted, or was it too far gone now? It certainly felt that way when Abelgadar spoke only days ago. He kept going over and over it in his head: how he would respond, could he be rescued, at what point should he run, would he even get the chance, was he leading his friends into certain death? Hussein would not hesitate, and the police would have weapons. He was saved from further angst by Ali asking him to play chess.

Chapter 30

Samir need not have worried. On Wednesday morning, 3rd July, it happened. Hussein called the trio together and in a quiet matter-of-fact manner gave them a simple instruction.

'Get ready. You have fifteen minutes. The mission is now. Wear dark, loose clothing. You must be ready to fight and move fast. Say your prayers. *Allahu Akbar.*' (God is most great).

The shock was enormous after all this time of waiting all cooped up. All remained static, transfixed as if rooted to the floor. Ali and Abdullah moved first, Samir slower, his brain trying to form some kind of plan as to how to warn those watching for him in advance. No plan came to mind; he was stuck with having to run both of his hands twice through his hair as he left the safe house. He would have to hope that the watchers were alert and themselves had back-up, and quick. Hussein was waiting at the door as they gathered. Moving out swiftly, another vehicle cruised slowly down the street, a white Ford transit van with four men inside. Hussein beckoned to the driver to pull in behind their own light brown Vauxhall Astra estate car. Two passengers jumped from the van as the rear doors opened. A third passed to Hussein what looked like homemade incendiary devices, which he deposited them in the back of the Astra. The exercise took less than a minute.

There was panic in the watching Met police car, an unmarked grey Vauxhall Insignia. Bellamy was the driver, with Detective Constable Jill Johnson in the back. The front-seat passenger, Detective Sergeant Patterson, was frantically calling in the situation.

'Monroe, Monroe, urgent. The equipment's just been dropped off. They're on the move. White Ford transit van and Astra estate. Need back-up, urgent. Repeat: need back-up.' After providing the registration number, they were off, keeping a safe distance.

Seconds later, Monroe was on, 'Patterson, where are you?'

'At the moment we are heading towards the Mile End Road, at a leisurely pace sir. Problem is, I don't want to be seen but don't want to lose them either.'

'OK, Patterson. I'm in a car right now and can be over there in five minutes and can mobilise back-up as we speak. Which vehicle is the group in?'

'The Astra, I don't know who is in the van, any ideas, sir?'

'No idea. We've had no intelligence at all on that one. Someone's been very quiet, or they're from out of town – doesn't matter now. We've got to stop them before they strike. Trouble is where the hell are they heading?'

Patterson had a question, 'we're coming up to the Mile End Road soon. How far away are you, because we can't follow both vehicles?'

Monroe replied, 'You stay with the Astra, because we'll all be at the job centre tomorrow if they get away. I'm not far away now on Whitechapel Road.'

'Right, OK, sir. They're just turning left onto the A11 Mile End Road, heading west towards the city. Hold on, they've speeding up. I think we've been spotted. Getting faster, do we stay with them, sir? We'll need the blue light?'

Monroe shouted, 'Of course you stay with

them! There are more cars on the way, with stingers and stuff. Who's your driver?'

'Bellamy. He's as good a driver as Lewis Hamilton.'

'He'd better be, Patterson. He'd better be.'

There was less interchange as they chased the two speeding vehicles down the Mile End Road, Bellamy staying rigidly focused on his task. The blue light and police siren alerted traffic in both directions, and drivers in panic turned off or drove up onto kerbs to get out of the way of the two fugitive vehicles driving at breakneck speed. Several minor accidents occurred: an elderly man collapsed, clinging to the sign at the pedestrian crossing he was about to negotiate. A man exiting the Blind Beggar public house stared in amazement at the speeding motorcade, shook his head, turned and walked back into the pub.

The Astra suddenly hung a sharp left. Patterson picked up the mike.

'The Astra's gone left. It looks like they're heading south, in the direction of the river.'

Monroe replied, 'Keep with them. We're further along the Mile End Road. We should pick up the transit any time now.'

The Astra continued at speed, careering

along the road, oblivious to anything in its path, the driver wildly swinging the steering wheel while frantically checking the rear-view mirror for sight of the flashing blue light close enough to prevent escape.

The other occupants were now in panic.

Ali was first to crack. 'What are we going to do, man? They're bound to catch us soon.'

Abdullah tried to sound brave. 'They would have tried to overtake by now if they wanted. Maybe they are waiting for back-up and another car will block us from the front.'

Samir's comment never materialised as Hussein roared from the driver's seat, 'Enough! Let me drive. I think I know where we have a chance of losing them.'

No one appeared convinced, but hope was always better than despair. At that moment all of Allah's soldiers said a silent prayer. The Astra rolled on. It had a mind of its own. Seconds felt like minutes; a minute felt like an eternity as they ploughed on. They were now near the river somewhere.

Samir was nervous. He had not said anything for some time. He needed to do something, but what? It felt like they were fleeing now with no intention of getting to an intended target. Hussein made a sharp left and then right and then left again. Ali and Abdullah in the back were not wearing seat belts and were thrown about like rag dolls. The police car was not in sight, but the siren could be heard wailing away. The car suddenly stopped in some kind of warehouse yard. They could see the dock and the water only yards away.

Hussein suddenly lunged. Samir felt a sharp pain in his side, and then another, higher up this time. Feeling trapped, he fumbled to undo his seatbelt and felt blood.

He had been stabbed! The Sword of Allah had been drawn again.

Hussein screamed, 'I knew you were a traitor. Get out of the car, infidel!'

Samir was already fainting, helpless. The door was opened and Hussein pushed him out onto the tarmac, and then the Astra sped off, tyres screeching, throwing mud and debris in its wake.

The police car roared into the yard with lights flashing and siren wailing just as Samir groggily tried to get to his feet. Up ahead, the Astra skidded right, around a corner of the warehouse and out of sight.

Bellamy stopped the Vauxhall Insignia, and Patterson and Detective Constable Jill Johnson jumped out to check on Samir. He was conscious, but his eyes were blank and unseeing.

Patterson swiftly barked orders, 'Stay here. See what you can do. Get an ambulance, fast! He's fading.'

Jumping back in the car Patterson said, 'get a move on, Bellamy. Don't lose them now!'

Bellamy floored the accelerator pedal and the big Vauxhall leaped forward, rounding the corner just in time to see the Astra in mid-air before it nose-dived into the murky black waters of the dock.

'Oh, sweet Jesus,' Patterson muttered. 'The shit's really hit the fan now.'

Bellamy brought the Vauxhall to a stop, and silence prevailed as the bubbles slowly subsided over the sunken Astra.

Tears flowed as Detective Constable Jill Johnson tended to Samir, unable to do anything but watch his life-blood ebbing away onto the muddy concrete of the dockyard.

Chief Inspector Monroe's luck was not much better. The white transit van had turned off before reaching the waiting police team.

Having traced the number plate given initially by Patterson, it turned out be cloned, actually belonging to a Toyota MX5 convertible registered to a nurse from Ipswich. Slowing down, the van was easily absorbed into the traffic as one of hundreds of similar vehicles on the roads of London on any given work day.

The break came when a call was received that a white Ford transit van had driven up Joiner Street to London Bridge Station entrance. Two men had got out, carrying incendiary devices that later turned out to be petrol bombs. These were hurled into the station and forecourt and thrown against the windows of the Shard building. The windows of the Shard building easily withstood the onslaught. The travelling public were less fortunate: two died instantly and twenty-five were injured, three dying later from their injuries. Escaping down London Bridge Street, luck ran out for the van fugitives, when a double-decker bus pulled out in front of them. They were driving way too fast to avoid a collision, and slammed straight into the back of the bus. As they emerged from the van, bloodied and staggering around the street, they were easily apprehended by two British Transport policemen and held for the brief time it took for the Met to arrive and bundle them into a police van.

Back in the dock yard, Detective Sergeant Patterson was briefing Chief Inspector Monroe as they waited for lifting gear and frogmen to arrive to retrieve the Astra from the dock. As an ambulance arrived in record time to take Samir to the hospital, an alert came through calling them back to the station. Leaving Bellamy, Johnson and other police officers to supervise the recovery of the Astra, they returned to Kensington police station.

The alert was about a man fitting Hussein's description, who had been seen running away from the dock yard at about the time of the incident. He had been picked up by beat detectives, who were currently tailing him on the underground, waiting for further instructions. It was not immediately regarded as urgent, as Hussein was at the bottom of the dock.

An hour later, after Monroe had been congratulated on the one hand for the apprehension of the van fugitives and less so for the non-apprehension of the occupants of the Astra, he was back with Patterson in his office, going through the events of the day in detail.

A red-faced detective constable burst into the office.

'You need to take this call right away, sir,' he stammered and moved away from the impending explosion.

It was Jill Johnson from the dockyard. 'You're not going to believe this, sir. There are only two bodies in the Astra!'

Monroe fell back into his chair, ashen-faced.

Patterson was concerned, 'Are you all right, sir? What on earth's the matter?'

Monroe handed him the phone.

'Jill, what is it?'

'We only found two bodies in the Astra!'

Monroe had recovered by now and barked at Patterson, 'It must be Hussein in the underground. He must have somehow jumped before the car went over into the dock. Grab him now, now, now!'

Meanwhile, at Whitechapel underground station, Hussein was nearing the top of the escalator. As he checked behind him, he saw two men running past other passengers at the bottom of the escalator. He ran to the exit, where he slowed and walked out, merging into the multitude outside.

Breathing heavily from their efforts, the two detectives emerged into the bright sunshine, standing for a moment whilst donning sunglasses. One went left towards the Blind Beggar pub, the other right, in the direction of the petrol station. Each man walked purposefully, looking left to right from the Asian shops to roadside stalls. As they were approaching the traffic lights a quarter of a mile away, each stopped and spoke into microphones clipped onto their lapels. Simultaneously, a tall, well-built Asian man with a beard stepped out from a stall selling mobile phones, iPhones and the like, close to the station entrance. The man, without a glance, strolled casually over to the entrance to Whitechapel underground and disappeared inside.

the target was? Did we win, or was it all a waste of time?'

Monroe replied in emphatic tones, 'It most definitely was not a waste of time. We prevented many more deaths of innocent people. Who was actually behind it all? It must be Abelgadar? What the target actually was, well—'

The Gent broke in. 'No. Abelgadar only thought he was the mastermind, but it was really Hussein. He is the Al Qaeda man.'

'How can you be so sure?' asked Spinner.

'Well, I can't be positive, but my doubts about Abelgadar were first raised when you told me your information from the Middle East was that he only became a firebrand cleric after his disastrous time in Bahrain.

'Your efforts to trace his background came to nought: not unexpected given the history of Iraq over the last two decades. Even if the names given were not faked, they could now be dead, if not killed by Saddam then by US forces. As for the authenticity of documentation, we know he travelled through Egypt, for example. Cairo would be just the place to acquire the appropriate fake documents virtually to order. I think it entirely possible that Hussein reports to someone other than Abelgadar, and was assigned to watch him just as much as to protect him. The fact that he appears to make his own rules and lives where he chooses supports this, as does Monroe's information about him visiting Western Union branches on a weekly basis, which in turn suggests that he had a regular supply of funds. Quite easy, really, when all you need to collect money from Western Union is some form of ID, and a password from the sender which can be texted from virtually anywhere in the world.

'Al Qaeda is a chameleon. One of its major strengths is its flexibility. It is like a virus that attaches itself to anything it chooses in order to pursue its cause to disrupt the West. It does not matter to them; whatever target was chosen or for whatever reason, so long as the headlines read 'Al Qaeda', they will always win!'

There was silence as the meeting mulled over this statement. Yes, they had caught the perpetrators, most of whom had lost their lives for their endeavours, to be rewarded in heaven as heroes. However, what the intended target or targets were remained unknown. Unfortunately, Al Qaeda still got their headlines.

Hours later, all media and news channels headlined with: *Al Qaeda plot on London thwarted.*

The group meditation swiftly ended as Monroe's mobile and pager sounded simultaneously. He was wanted by both media and his boss at the Met, but the latter took precedence. The meeting broke up and they went their separate ways, all promising to be in touch soon. They were ushered out through a back door, leaving Monroe after the OK from his boss to go out front to face the TV news and press, who stood, cameras at the ready, anxious for a statement to meet their deadlines.

Monroe did not disappoint. Taking a deep breath and with a bit of a swagger, he went out to face the cameras and lights. 'Ladies and gentlemen, I can give you a general statement, but any further details beyond what I am about to say will have to wait until forensics have done their job.

'A coded message, which we believe to be genuine, has been received by the Daily Express from Al Qaeda, claiming responsibility for the petrol bombing in the London Bridge Quarter earlier today, in which five members of the public died and twenty more were injured. This was part of a much larger terrorist plot to bomb and wreak havoc on a target in another part of the Capital. Four perpetrators have been apprehended, and three others have unfortunately died in the process – two when their vehicle sank in the waters of a Thames side dock and one other at the hands of another gang member. By thwarting this evil terrorist plot, we have prevented the deaths of many more innocent people and saved others from serious injury.'

The next week, when the fuss had died down and headlines had become third-page news only, a handful of people would understand the significance of Monroe's words and how important the timing had been in thwarting the plot, for in the two days following that meeting in Kensington police station on 3rd July, certain events needed to be considered.

4th July 2012: American Independence Day. There is a Picnic at the US Ambassador's residence, Winfield House in Regents Park.

An item on the US Embassy website and reproduced with a video on YouTube, read:

It is more than three thousand miles from Washington DC to London, but the distance didn't stop more than fifteen-hundred Diplomats, embassy staff, local dignitaries, and friends from celebrating American Independence Day in the heart of London. The US Embassy London's July 4th Family Picnic was hosted at Ambassador Susman's official residence, Winfield House. The celebration included a presentation by the embassy's Marines, music, games like tug-o-war and, of course, hamburgers.

5th July 2012: Opening of the Shard Building

by His Excellency Sheikh Hamad Bin Jassem Bin Jabor Al Thani, Prime Minister and Minister of Foreign Affairs of the State of Qatar and Prince Andrew Albert Christian Edward, the Duke of York, third child and second son of Queen Elizabeth II and currently fourth in line to throne.

5th July 2012: An article appeared in the Independent newspaper, the first three paragraphs read:

The British Museum is no longer just for the British, it seems. As government funding falls and the museum seeks other sources of cash, the UK's most popular visitor attraction has more exhibitions on tour than ever before and is increasingly targeting wealthy countries. The museum has sent artefacts to Abu Dhabi, Australia, Japan and China in the past year, and is planning a major collaboration in India. Neil MacGregor, the museum's director, said: 'Because it is a global collection, it is now being used across the globe.'

A week or so later, a young blonde lady and a gentleman teed off at Forest View Golf Club in Cheshire. Both managed respectable if not remarkable first shots, and strode off purposely up the fairway of the first hole. The Lady turned to the Gent and said, 'How did you go on with Amelia's stalker, then?'

'Ah! Did I not tell you? Since the boss at the gallery had a quiet word, he has been in but kept a very low profile. Amelia is still very concerned, as his eyes are daggers whenever he makes eye contact. The Willi Kissmer exhibition opens in two weeks and she has asked me to be there and try to suss him out and perhaps have my own word if necessary.'

'Good idea,' the young blonde confirmed.

Following behind and observing were two middle-aged men, both veteran golfers. Jon, first on the tee, was setting up for his swing.

Jim, his partner that morning, commented, 'Body language, Jon, what do you think, eh?

Are they an item, then, eh?'

'Yeah maybe they are Jon.'

Jim tried again, 'Why do you think that, then, Jon?'

'Jim, you're putting me off my swing.'

'Sorry, Jon, but they don't have any rings on or anything, do they?'

'Will you fucking keep quiet?'

'Sorry, Jon, I only meant...'

'Fuck, you might as well tee off first now. I've lost it with all you're chattering!'

Printed in Great Britain
by Amazon